hallucination

a novel

kim green

hallucination

BookLogix Publishing Services
Alpharetta, Georgia

ISBN 978-1-61005-111-8

Library of Congress Control Number: 2011919589

Cover Art: D. Lammie Hanson

Cover Design: Jim deBarros and Patrick Malloy

Printed in the United States of America.

Dedication

hallucination is dedicated to my Father, Robert James Green; my Mother, Mary Ellen Green; my Son, Micah London Foster and to music for allowing me the privilege of knowing how awesome and effortless true love can be.

Prologue

Almost dying is mere flirtation. Almost dying leaves you awkward and restless. Not knowing where you belong; with the living or with the dead. I sit in this conundrum, operating with the benign numbness of the dead and the constant turmoil of the living.
Only now do I stumble over my dead; writing for forgiveness.

PART ONE

Scattered Seeds

CHAPTER 1 | *Prophesy*

New York City, 1981

"**N**o she didn't!"

"**N**o she didn't."

"**N**o she didn't..."

I wept and screamed and pounded my fists into her. The weary nurse appeared fat but her middle was girded, making it easier for my fists to release the pain caused by her words. She was a punching bag. I was being trained for *Life*.

After enduring my frantic blows, the nurse asked me if I wanted to see her body. "No," I said with unusual certainty. I didn't want the image of my dead mother lingering in my mind's eye, forever. Although I congratulated myself for "smart thinking" for a 15-year old, I didn't realize that by avoiding the visual, her ghost would continue to haunt.

The nurse took me into a yellow waiting room with peeling paint, a neglected tile floor littered with graying gum wads, cloudy fast food wrappers, tattered newspapers, and cigarette butts. Some of the butts were encircled with faded red lipstick, just like my mother's. I looked around hoping that she would be sitting there, but she wasn't.

After a few more minutes the nurse led me into a messy office, so I could make phone calls and spill the news. I called my father, Roy, then my grandmother, Biggs, and Aunt Perris in Wisconsin. Last, I called my best friend, Allegra, who screamed. I was numb. They all had answered the phone with the same gentle innocence. "Hello?"

"Mom died," I said, the bearer of the worst possible news.

Roy's voice quietly trembled. In utter disbelief, all he could say was, "Whaaat..." the end of the word losing steam as he sighed into it. My grandmother, Biggs, shrieked while Aunt Perris took the phone from her. I could hear my grandmother grabbing at things that could not support her, causing her to tumble and stumble towards the floor. I could hear the sound of objects falling around her.

Aunt Perris said into the phone, "Mari's gone?" I couldn't answer her. The nurse took the phone from my tensed grip. I could no longer understand what was happening to me.

The nurse said to Aunt Perris, "Hello. I'm so sorry for your family's loss. Yes...her daughter's okay. Miss Marigold suffered a heart attack on the subway." The nurse listened to Aunt Perris and then she said, "Yes, yes, the daughter will be taken home. Yes, she is alone...Again, I'm sorry for your loss." She hung up the phone and turned to me. I was looking down at the filthy tile, too weak to lift my head.

The nurse took me to meet the police officer who would drive me to my empty home. In the squad car, I squirmed in his mess. I was a lawful citizen who had just become a motherless daughter. I was frightened by the crumbs and dirt, hoping that none of it would touch me. I was still wearing my navy uniform and my brown loafers from the school day. Mommy would have been mad that I hadn't taken my school clothes off as soon as I got home. My penny loafers brushed over his used coffee cups, candy wrappers, and police debris. The copper pennies on my shoes shone amid the mess. The dispatcher's radio blared, filling in our silence. My mind drifted in and out. The dispatcher's codes lacked any trace of humanity. The voice from the console was robotic and cruel as it nonchalantly reported the tragedies of the day. The officer turned down the volume, as if embarrassed by the cruelty of things.

When he pulled up in front of my high-rise apartment building on 5th Avenue, he seemed sad as he helped pull my traumatized self out of the front seat. He stood outside on the passenger side as he stammered, "Are you going to be OK from here?" I said nothing, not clear how I could be OK from this moment on.

"Thanks for the ride," I managed to whisper.

"No problem," he said.

"Bye," I said. I lingered, not ready to face what awaited.

"Bye," the officer said, not wanting to let go either.

I watched him get back into his side of the car. The coldness of February whipped around me, leading me into my new abyss.

I entered the heavy glass doors that led to the lobby and saw my father waiting for me on an iron bench. He was looking down at his knees and rubbing his hands along the creases in his pants. When he saw me, he hugged me so hard that I could feel his moist face sinking into the nerves in my neck. He lingered as if he was waiting to disappear. I, too, wanted to vanish from the brick-hard reality that had just knocked us down. My mother was dead.

Silently, my father and I took the elevator to the fourth floor to enter what used to be my home. We walked among the ruins of the kitchen. The refrigerator door still ajar, the aluminum foil that I had just ripped was still on the countertop and the Tupperware containers were still waiting to be opened. I had been preparing a surprise dinner of last night's leftovers. It had been chicken cacciatore – with extra mushrooms, just like I liked it. When the police called, I was just about to turn on the oven, remembering her list of safety measures. *Wrap the chicken carefully in tin foil. You can add the sauce; the foil will hold it in.* She had taught me how to re-heat leftovers in order to help out more. Her duties as a single mother had been wearing on her. I wanted to please her that night.

"I just can't believe she's gone," Roy said into the air. I said nothing as I busied my hands throwing the leftovers and their Tupperware containers into the trashcan.

Roy closed the refrigerator door. I started to put the aluminum foil into the trash when he interrupted. "What you doin', Ava? Don't waste that. You don't know what you're doing. I know you're sad. But life goes on," he said.

I held the long box of foil that my mother had touched so many times before. With tears streaming down my face I said, "Now what?"

"Now, nothin'," my father spat.

Marigold Jaspers was born in Atlanta, but was moved, as a child, to Wisconsin. It was my mother's craving to escape the blandness of both the South and the Midwest that flowed through her veins. She yearned to don the cape of urbane sophistication. It had been her dream to 1) come to New York City 2) become a model 3) marry a rich man and 4) have a daughter who would attend 5) a single-sex private school. After arriving in New York, she became a runway model but didn't make any real money from it so she pursued Daddy instead. He wasn't rich but he was the richest man my mother had ever met. The "daughter" that she conjured up was me, Ava Morgan Blackmon. The single-sex private school that she sent me to was Eastside Girls Academy, which is where I gained my insatiable appetite for knowledge and material things, and my excruciating discomfort with anything unclean. Thus, the reason I itch today.

According to my holistic doctor, Dr. Lazard, my mother's fatal heart attack on the New York City subway was one of the great "shocks" of my life and the reason for my mildly irritated kidneys. Dr. Lazard said our kidneys hold and process the hurt and the pain in our lives. Nothing can protect the kidneys when a 15-year-old girl loses her mother on the New York City subway on a Monday night while preparing a surprise dinner for her.

The night of her death, my father paced back and forth from the bedroom to the living room as if he was looking for her, but finding only her remnants. She left her bed unmade with a tattered pair of pantyhose dangling off the side of the bed. The frantically ripped new package laid with her promise that she would clean up when she got home. "Y'all were in a rush," he whispered audibly. I was embarrassed by Mommy's mess.

The two of us were not alone. After the word got out from one Eastside girl to the next, several of my best friends had been sent in cabs to share my first motherless night. Eastside Girls Academy was the exclusive private school on the Upper East Side that Marigold bragged about to anyone who would listen. In a sentence, Eastside cost $15,000 a year, the families all consisted of millionaire fathers, lunching mothers, and spoiled little rich girls, and me – a smart black girl who was lucky enough to be there on academic scholarship.

I left my father alone to make small talk with my friends as they huddled together in our living room, searching for words for a broken friend. The rich girls sat obediently in a row, watching me from the sofa as though I was on a foreign television show and they couldn't grasp the plot. I sat in a side chair, away from them.

"Thanks for coming out in the cold, you guys," I broke the ice.

None of them said anything. They stared blankly at me as though they were staring into something they couldn't recognize – *misfortune*.

I was distracted by the sound of my father pacing and rummaging and searching for something he wouldn't find. The apartment rang loudly with the sound of death. It was as if the buzzing of a mothered life and the sound of giggling teenaged girls had never happened there. *But I know it did.*

The last time that Roy came out of the bedroom, he came to say goodnight to us. He spoke as if we were alone. "Tomorrow, I'll go to the funeral home to make the arrangements."

"Can I go?" I heard myself say without my permission.

"No, it's gonna be too much for you. I'll take care of it. Ya Mama wants to be cremated, but you know I don't agree with that..." he said with his big eyes, showing his constant disdain.

"Do what she wants, Daddy," I said.

"Good night," he said. "I will."

"Thank you," I said for Marigold.

Roy hugged me first, while each of the Eastside girls waited their turn to hesitantly hug my father. He said, weakly, "Thank y'all for coming." With tears in his eyes he said, "Good night." He slammed the door to my mother's room that they had shared when I was little and before the hitting began.

After he went to bed, we all sat in silence except for me tapping my foot against the wooden leg of the brown velvet armchair. I could hear my father in my mother's bedroom on the phone calling his sister and brother, telling our news. I looked at my friends and they each offered tender teenage condolences.

"I'm so sorry, Ava. "

"I love you."

"I'm here for you, whatever you need."

"I don't know what to say..."

When I heard my father switching off the bathroom light, I knew he had made his last call of the night. He would spend the rest of the night distracted by her smell on the pillowcase. Allegra, Chloe, Daniela, and Pietra had each asked if they could call their mothers to say goodnight. My stomach fell as I heard each of them say into the phone, "Mom?" I stood alone in a new type of loneliness.

The louvered doors that Marigold insisted on barely transformed the space that was intended to be a dining room, into an almost private bedroom. It faced into the small living room where we all sat like mummies. After speaking to their mothers, Pietra, Chloe, and Daniela eventually sprawled out on the aging dark brown carpet, without sheets, blankets, or pillows. Allegra and I would sleep in my room. Me on the twin bed, she beside me on the trundle bed, the louvered doors open so we could all seem together.

As soon as the lights were off, three of them fell asleep, exhausted with the rigors of reality. Allegra and I lay wide awake in silence. She caressed my hand all night long, not knowing what else to say or do.

Because my mother dabbled in Christian Science which demanded that she rely solely on God, she gave up on all material means of healing, including doctors and the pills that they pushed. My mother cared for her high blood pressure with music, positive thoughts, vodka, and cigarettes.

After the divorce, Roy had moved out of the 5th Avenue apartment and into the depths of Harlem. "Harlem is where I belong," Roy used to tell me, showing his relief that he had finally escaped the decorated life of Marigold's insistence. There was nowhere for my father to turn when it was time to make funeral arrangements.

Marigold only rarely attended the Christian Science services at Lincoln Center's Unity Church, where the rest of the week, the "pulpit" was the stage for the world's most famous jazz and ballet performances. Roy shied away from even attempting to navigate the lily-white congregation. "Those people are simply not my kind of people," Roy would say from time to time. "Your mother loved *those* people."

Roy had started attending a storefront church in Harlem "with a woman-preacher," as he described her. "She's a woman, but she sure can preach. I *like* her," Roy used to say with a chauvinist's warmth. The church was located on 125th street and Lenox Avenue, above a sneaker store. Roy improvised as he decided that was where the funeral would be. The eulogy was performed by the "woman-preacher" whom my mother had never met. I sat in the front row of folding chairs completely numbed by the debacle that was Marigold Blackmon's closing ceremony. *She would have died if she had been there.*

The makeshift church was packed with white girls who had never been allowed to go to Harlem and had surely never attended a "storefront church" above a sneaker store. They came in packs of yellow cabs and climbed the rickety stairs to the musty makeshift church. They came to pay their respects to a small golden urn that held "Ava's-mom-who-died," as they referred to her amongst themselves. Marigold would have been impressed that so many daughters of millionaires came all the way to Harlem just to say goodbye.

After the hazy funeral, I went back to the apartment with my EGA friends, friends from my father's job, and people from the building. Surprisingly, Marigold's friends stayed away, too scared to face the atrocity of untimely death. Everyone who came to grieve stayed a little longer, before they would forget. Only Roy and I would have to live with this loss sitting in the center of our lives like a statue.

The apartment had been filled with food by neighbors while we were above the sneaker store. Roy scolded me about the glazed lemon cake that I devoured, slice by slice, as if it had been baked just for me. Roy watched me from the corner of his eye as he greeted the guests and robotically thanked everyone for coming. The Eastside girls finally left and I was alone with the last slices of the cake, while my father still entertained those who lingered, piled into our tiny apartment, pretending to be grieving when they were just passing time.

I squatted down in the small space between the dining room table and the stereo cabinet. The 45 on the turntable was "Fashion" by David Bowie. I played it over and over again just like Marigold would have. Music was always her escape. The remains of the cake and I were close enough to the stereo for me to be able to put the needle back at the beginning of the record every three minutes, before the needle noisily skidded across the grooves. The crowd grew and thinned. I was oblivious in my sugar haze with only the sound of David Bowie's funky insistence soothing me. I felt like Marigold, held by the music and floating above everything that hurt.

When everyone had left and it was just us, I moved slowly, helping my father clean up. He came over to the empty cake pan and growled, "Ava did you eat all of that cake by yourself?"

I looked away and said, "Yes."

"You never listen! Diabetes runs in our family. You never listen. You need to listen sometimes! You've got a hard head!" He slammed the door and went to mom's room.

David Bowie had gone off for the final time. I kneeled down again to put the needle back to the beginning.

CHAPTER 2 | *Due Diligence*

After the funeral, I took my sadness and quietly morphed into a spooky goblin-like character that sad kids, like me, called "Goth." Dressing like a ghoul and listening to dark music, I took on the persona of the living dead. My costume was black from head-to-toe with flea market rosary beads around my neck, crucifixes in my ears and black nail polish on my fingers and toes. I was buried beneath the layers of my mourning.

They had waited to have me. Marigold was 34 and Roy was 44 when I was born. The stresses of Marigold's subway death and the prospect of raising me alone at 60 years old were too much for him. Roy's internal rage flared. Daddy's smile was big and white and that of a rabid animal looking for anything small he could devour. Once the feelings of his prey had been chewed up and swallowed by his words, he would feel strong again.

Roy's problem was that he was born in 1922. The ruthless racism that he endured in the army did it to him. The indignities that he had suffered as a black high school graduate with only the strength of his hands as his resume, made for perpetual rage. Roy was embittered at all of the EGA fathers whom he swore were being paid millions to sit behind glass desks and read the newspaper. Roy was proud, never dignifying them with his envy.

My father's rage stank of pain; a powerful mix of stale cologne and over-bleached undershirts. He was constantly blowing up at me about my loud music, the dishes in the sink, or the laundry. His method of discipline was a worn brown leather belt that hung on the back of his bedroom door on a special hook.

A typical night went like this:

"Ava, come in here and do these dishes!" he would bellow from outside of his bedroom door.

"Coming."

"When?"

"I'm doing something."

"*Something* needs to wait. Come in here, Ava, I'm not playin' with you."

"I'm *coming*." I was annoyed.

"Come *now*, Ava. I am not playin' with you."

As I would emerge from my room, he always stood much taller than usual, the brown leather belt dangling from his slightly gnarled arthritic hand.

"You never listen, Ava!" His voice neared shrill. "That's why I have to use this. When you learn to listen..." His voice would fade, knowing that I knew the rest. Then came the swat like a crack of lightning across my black sweat pants, which shielded me from the leather's full impact. *It still stung.* Without dignity, I jumped to flee from the shame of being spanked as a teenager. "You're just like ya mama!" he would say over and over again, as he slammed the door. I would turn up the music. *I loved and hated him so much.*

While I washed the dinner dishes, I used the hottest water possible, turning my palms blood red, boiling inside. As I scrubbed the food off the yellow plates, I would curse under my breath through the steam that was shielding my tears. I glared at the melting food, shivering at how ugly it becomes; dripping, drooling, and morphing into something grotesque.

I was mad at her for leaving me with him. I spitefully took her side, wishing that she would have taken me wherever she went. I prayed to get away from him. I prayed to graduate from high school, quickly. I prayed to be free. I prayed for someone to pray to.

Rage wasn't just Roy's alone. I also raged. Music was my hideout. The louder I played it, the angrier Roy became. We had both become deaf and dumb. Most mornings, by 10, I could be found at Eastside Girls Academy slumped against the wall opposite the lockers, sleeping. I was usually hung over with exhaustion after a night of half-done homework, arguing with Roy and hiding behind eerie gothic tunes that filled my closet-less cubicle of a bedroom.

I completed the last two years of high school using the methods of my privileged white girl peers. I ingested handfuls of diet pills, diuretics, laxatives, and caffeine every morning as my breakfast to cope with my dormant misery. My friends and I all toyed with bulimia to make us feel like we were living the glamorous lives of the fashion models that hung on our walls that we all worshipped. The only problem was that I couldn't bring myself to actually throw anything up. Wasting food was a sin to Roy who was raised "po'" in South Carolina. I settled for mental anorexia as my default.

The teachers took notice of my dozing off in class and in the halls. There were countless closed-door conferences about me; with and without me.

"Ava, how are things?" the school counselor, an older white woman with smudged red lipstick, would ask me every week at our assigned meeting time.

"OK," I usually said.

"How's your father? Are you two coping with everything during this very difficult time?"

"Yeah, it's OK," I would say again, staring at the red smudge stains on her yellowing teeth.

"How is *he* handling things?" she would probe.

"We argue a lot, that's all."

"About what?" the red lips and teeth would inquire sweetly.

"Chores. Staying up too late. My music. "

"What do you mean argue?" said the counselor.

"The regular stuff. He lectures a lot. Sometimes he spanks me...a little," I stuttered. The smudged red lips turned down in a frown.

"Ava does that happen often?" she asked.

The pea green office walls started to close in on us. I was torn between telling and not telling. I took the middle ground. "Not often," I lied. "Just sometimes, when he's really mad."

"How does he sppaank you?" she asked with mild terror in her voice.

"Just with a belt...an old belt," I clarified. "It's actually soft," I corrected.

"Hmmm...Thank you, Ava, for sharing. Get back to class. See you next week."

The next week, two sets of red smudged lips were waiting for me. The counselor and my homeroom teacher. Three was a crowd.

"Ava, we are going to assist you and your father in coping with your loss. We are recommending an intervention. I will call your father with the details. You both will attend appointments with a family therapist that the school works with. He will assist you two in getting used to the loss of your mother and teach you better ways to live together."

"How much will it cost? You know my father won't pay for anything extra."

"There's no cost. Eastside Girls Academy works with this team of doctors all the time. It's an arrangement that we have."

I was surprised that anyone else at EGA had problems.

With her usual stiffness, my pasty homeroom teacher touched my shoulder with a dry five-finger brush that sent chills up my spine and through my thin cotton blouse. "It's going to be OK, Ava. You're a good student. We all believe in you."

It was determined soon after the weekly evening meetings started that Roy would stop hitting me. The belt lay in eerie repose on the singular hook on the back of his bedroom door, only stirring when he would slam the door to end our conversations. It had been said that if there were further problems, EGA would have to remove me from the home to live with another school family. I secretly dreamed of landing on Park Avenue with a maid serving me every night and a chauffeur who would drive me and my new family to our country house on the weekends.

Roy said, "You're not going to live with some rich white folks so that they can say that I couldn't care for my own child. That's what they think of black people, anyway. Hell no!" he raged. "I'll take you out of that white school if I have to. The only reason I keep you there is because that's what your crazy mama wanted." Roy was always angry, possessive, and obsessive about her. He loved her and resented her with all his might.

In my dreams, Marigold would come to me. I could see her through the slats in my louvered doors, dancing to her music. I would wake up in a cold sweat, wishing and missing and crying myself back to sleep. Marigold's scent of citrus mixed with vodka and cigarettes seeped out of the "French eggshell" white walls into my dreams.

"Mom are you coming to the dance concert?"

"I'll try to make it, but if it's too late, I'll miss it. You know I have to work late to get overtime."

"Just this once. Please come. I choreographed three dances. Daddy's coming."

"I'll try," she'd lie.

Another time, "Mom can you come to my soccer game?"

"Ava it's in the middle of the day. You know I can't make that."

"Daddy's coming."

"He can. He has a government job. I work on Wall Street. It's different. Don't make me feel bad," she'd say. "I'll make it up to you. I'll make Turkey Tettrazini." *She always seduced with food.*

"Mommy, are you coming to the parents meeting at Pietra's house?"

"I'm not feeling well and besides I can't get off in time."

I so desperately wanted the other mothers to see her. She was beautiful to every eye. Marigold's features were delicate, her smile hypnotic. Her exotic Native American cheekbones were a daily reminder of the drunkard father she never knew. Marigold didn't come to Eastside often. She stayed away like wealth was a contagious and deadly disease. There was too much pressure to look like the other mothers; the mothers who lunched and got professional manicures. She was embarrassed by her off-the-sale-rack clothes from Macy's and her side-of-the-bed manicures that she gave herself after her third drink on Sunday nights. The other mothers were always seen in clothes designed by Gucci and Yves St Laurent. Marigold only wore shame.

Mommy and I simply didn't have the crucial accoutrements of East Coast wealth that became our silent obsessions. These items included, a super-sized apartment ("The Classic 7" it was called – meaning 7 rooms: 2 bathrooms, 1 kitchen, 1 living room, 2 bedrooms, 1 den, which was always the library), a larger country house, a housekeeper, and membership to a country club. Although my mother and I never spoke about these items aloud, visions of them danced in our heads. *Wanting* had become the centerpiece of our existence.

The liquor store 12 blocks away delivered a gallon of Vodka every Friday evening, without fail, to our doorman who would buzz our apartment to let her know the bottle was coming up like a male suitor. Every night of the week while she thought I was sleeping, Marigold would dutifully mix herself cocktails as if she were working the night shift. After the first cocktail, she would cross over. Without her knowing that I was spying on her, I would peek through my shuttered louvered doors and watch her doing model poses and standing in front of the full length mirror playing her favorite 45s like "Reminiscing" by the Little River Band, or Al Green's "Let's Stay Together," over and over and over and over and over again. She posed with her cocktails in front of the mirror as if she were selling regrets.

My bedroom doors gave me secret access to the sticky sounds of my mother's "dates" with herself. Her music mixed with cocktails would put her in another world where money was no object and she fit in. She would talk to herself, creating scenes where she too was boastful, pretentious, and taken care of. She would no longer shudder at talk of private planes, country estates, and butlers because she had them all.

I never knew how far away from reality her "happy hours" took her until my mother's childhood friend from Wisconsin, Maria, asked if her daughter, Garland, could come stay with us so she could go to beauty school to become a nail tech. Marigold had been thrilled with what she thought was a golden opportunity to influence another young black woman to aspire to "the finer things in life."

Garland, like my mother, also dreamed of a life far away from the boredom that was the Midwest. She was gorgeous with a porcelain complexion and reddish hair the color of shiny copper pennies that stretched down to the middle of her back. When Garland's hair was freshly hot-combed, it was a prize that hung down her back like a sheet of silk. Garland wore all the latest fashions, platform shoes, bell bottoms, and paisley tie-up blouses. I wanted to be like her and she wanted to be like me – *a New Yorker*. Garland living with us would give me the big sister that I always dreamed of. I loved her pretty name.

My mother sometimes worked night shifts as a data processor at Lehman Brothers. The days after those late shifts, mommy would always oversleep; arriving at Eastside disheveled, late and breathless. She was always the last mother there. I remember waiting, sitting in the hollow school on the cold tile stairs; waiting by the front door. Waiting. Waiting for her. *Embarrassed* by her. When Garland came to live with us, things changed. Like a savior, Garland always arrived every afternoon at 3:45, without fail. Sometimes she was early.

One evening, after dinner, Garland was finishing up the dishes; I was in my room doing my homework behind the louvered doors. My mother was in her room talking on the phone with Allegra's mother. My mother's door was open. She was only on her first drink. Garland overheard my mother speaking: "Yes, that's Garland, our new maid."

I heard a shrill scream from the kitchen. My stomach sank. She emerged from her room, drink in hand, cursing; "Stop that screaming. Can't you see that I'm on the damned phone?" Garland continued to scream. My mother quickly got Allegra's mom off the phone. I could hear her trying to reason with Garland.

"Garland – you know how people are in New York. It's just the way to get along with these people. Show them that you're just as good as they are."

"Miss Mari, how can you lie? I'm not your maid; I'm your best friend's daughter."

"They don't know that," my mother said.

"*I* know it, Ava knows it, but *you*, I don't even know *you* anymore," Garland yelled.

"Garland – don't speak to me like that, young lady. You'll never even meet that woman. What the hell does it matter?"

"Miss Mari, you won't have to worry about it. I'm going home, Saturday. I'm going to call my Mama and tell her what you did... what you *said*. You can explain the rest to your ex-best friend. I hate you, Miss Mari."

I moved closer to the louvered doors so I could hear more. I heard Garland hurling the yellow plates to the checkered tile floor. The apartment was so small that there was nowhere for any of us to run.

The next morning Garland said sadly, "Ava, I'm going home Saturday. I'm homesick. It's time for me to go back to what I'm used to."

On Saturday morning, Garland used her last 15 dollars to take a cab to LaGuardia airport. Maria had booked the flight. Garland was gone. She no longer idolized "rich Miss Marigold from New York."

Marigold's hangovers, lies, illusions, hopes, and dreams were meant to be a gift to me, but they became a curse. She left me with the ignorance to want what others have, without knowing what it is they *lacked.*

Superficiality never seeks due diligence.

CHAPTER 3 | *Cyclone*

New York City, 2003

After 22 years, the apartment was the same. Same décor. Same floors. Nothing had changed. The sameness made the walls feel restless, as if the air itself was dying for something new. The sadness of Marigold's death wouldn't fade. It was inside the walls, seeping through the paint. After all these years, the apartment still felt like someone was missing.

I nervously entered the apartment with the same key ring from childhood. I kept the "New York keys" on the same chain that Daddy had bought me in high school after I lost my keys on the bus and had to wait for him in the lobby for hours. Roy had chided my carelessness. "That was stupid," he said chuckling and rolling his eyes back in his head as he playfully hurt me.

When he heard the key click in the lock, I could hear his voice, "Ava – is that you?"

"Yes, Daddy, we're all here," I said as I peered behind the half open door. I was excited to see him. It had been a year.

Daddy was already standing and coming towards me and my family. As I hugged him, his smell was unchanged. I was greeted with his usual judgment. "Ava, why'd you come here lookin' so skinny? You look terrible!"

"Daddy, call me Morgan."

"You know I call you *Ava*. It's what ya Mama wanted when she named you."

I had dropped the name "Ava" when I started working in the music business. "Ava" sounded too privileged and too much like Marigold's twisted dreams. "Morgan" was stronger and simpler. *Down to earth.*

I had been sure to wear my New Yorker's uniform; black pants, black fitted T-shirt, and black medium-heeled shoes. My husband, Peter Holmes, was also in head-to-toe black with L.L. Bean shoes on his feet. Our nearly one-year-old daughter, Rain, was also wearing a black velour onesie, courtesy of Pietra, who had diligently researched and found black infant wear on the RockStar Baby website. The package had come to Oro Valley in an express mail pouch soon after the announcement of Rain's birth hit the EGA Alumnae newsletter. Her note read, "Here's to the baby of one of the coolest girls in school. She has to match her mom!"

"Peter, you look good. Real good. Now give me my granddaughter! Rain, you've gotten so big! Soon we'll have to find you a job!" Daddy always joked about Rain getting a job. My father was consumed with regret that I married a man without a degree, whom he decided could never take care of us after he was gone.

I smiled lightly at the job reference and tried to push them all out of my way in the cramped foyer and into the living room. I felt like I was going to fall over. Daddy walked in front of us, still complaining. "Ava, answer me - why do you look so skinny?" It was true. I had lost 30 pounds since the last time. My black capris were falling unfashionably off of my dwindling frame.

"Daddy, you know what the Eastside girls say, "you can never be too rich or too thin."

"Is that what all those skinny white girls told you? They have no idea what they're talkin' about. They've been eatin' cheese and crackers for dinner their whole lives. Take it from me, Baby Ava, you look terrible!"

Daddy had always said that about white people at whom he was perpetually annoyed. "They spend their money on boats, country houses, and maids and skimp on eatin'!" I chuckled at the memories of the three course meals he would prepare, despite the fact that I had been invited to dinner at a classmate's house. When I got home, I could smell the dinner from the hallway. He'd always ask, "So, what did you eat for dinner? Cheese and crackers?"

And I would say, laughing, "No! Tuna fish with cheese and crackers!" We both would cackle until our stomachs hurt.

Peter, as always, was on his best behavior when he was in the presence of Roy. He was very aware that my father never trusted him, his suburban upbringing, and his pipe dream of being a drummer. Peter was a construction worker when we met but he was once an aspiring drummer.

"Papa Blackmon, let me get these suitcases out of the way. Can I get you something from the kitchen?"

"No, thanks, Peter. Just take a load off. I know it's been a long day for y'all."

I could not wait to sit down while Roy played with Rain and Peter went into the kitchen to find something to eat. Traveling had worn me out. I wanted to fall asleep sitting up on the couch. I struggled to keep my eyes open while Rain crawled around Roy's house slippers. Roy kept saying to her, "Don't eat my toes! Stay off my feet!" Rain laughed while Roy beamed in a whole new way.

The long wait at the airport in Arizona had been awful. Rain cried when she needed to be changed and I pretended to ignore her because of the weakness that had settled into the crevices of my bones. Peter signaled to me across a row of seats with an angry wiggling finger, pointing at our tomato red diaper bag. As usual, he was on his cell phone talking to undisclosed acquaintances. I dragged myself out of my seat, scooped Rain off the floor with one arm and used the other to carry the diaper bag across the waiting area floor. I taped up the clean diaper without being as gentle as I should have. She whimpered.

I had packed too much in my carry-on. It was full of high heels and too many tops. I had packed a diaper bag bursting with diapers, a canister of wipes, jars of baby food, and too many toys. Peter had refused to carry the diaper bag. He once explained that "a man carrying a diaper bag had obviously been emasculated." Peter happily carried Rain on and off the plane while I dragged the bags.

Peter didn't know how bad I had been feeling. I hadn't told him. I told myself the stress of my job at the recording studio and a new baby were to blame for wearing my body down so far. Since my pregnancy, I had never felt quite myself. Roy would be furious that I wasn't feeling well, so I was determined not to tell him, either.

Growing up, whenever I was sick, Daddy would say it was my own fault, because I had been "stupid." I also knew that I wouldn't tell him that Peter and I were having problems. He would have launched into his canned lecture about me marrying a "dumb" drummer.

Daddy was complicated. He was hurtful and harsh most of the time. To him, everything was black vs. white; Jews vs. Christians; haves vs. have-nots, and the most important thing to know was that money rules the world. Roy was deaf to progress. Racism had caused a wound in him so deep that it never healed. Anger was his crutch, carrying him from one decade into the next.

Although he was hard to deal with, he was hell bent on doing whatever he thought would make me happy. His generosity was his way of saying sorry for the turbulence of *life after Marigold.* Daddy had been generous to a fault, causing everyone in the family to develop a perverse jealousy. They all hated him for loving me so much and they hated me for being the recipient of his showering love. Even Garland stopped speaking to us after she had grown up. She was still mad about what happened with Marigold when she came to New York for beauty school. As a family, Roy and I were together and apart.

As I grew, I came to understand Marigold's dilemma and her need to flee from Daddy's suffocating grip. As Daddy's daughter, I didn't have the same freedom she did to escape him with a simple court-ordered decree and a binding payment plan. Eventually, I sought freedom from Daddy in my own ways. I threw myself into anything that I could. After college, I ended up obsessing about work and play. For most of my adult years, I reveled in music, stayed out a little too late, drank a little too much, and found intoxication in the company of handsome men.

New York City, 1993

After too many years of self-inflicted debauchery and music business mayhem, I met Peter Holmes in Luis Muñoz Marin International Airport in San Juan, Puerto Rico. It was the start of Hurricane season. My trip had been cut short by gusty winds and threats of torrential rains. I was forced to leave the spa in Tortola a day earlier than planned. The flights were all either delayed or cancelled. The airport was packed with thousands of flights grounded in Puerto Rico, all of us trying to get back home, wherever that was. I had been stuck in the airport for hours already. Staring, reading, napping, tossing and turning in my uncomfortable seat was how I spent my hours as they dragged by. Awakening from a nap, I noticed Peter across the concourse travelling with a large group of overweight church ladies. It was a strange sight. He was such a striking vision. He had to be 6'5". His fair skin and bluish eyes startled me. I could see his eyes across the room. I was blinded by him. I had always loved exotic men who looked like that. They had always loved me back.

I sat up, fixed my lipstick and stared at him until he realized he was being summoned. His smooth creamy skin was like that of an angel. He had long luxurious eyelashes, wavy dark hair, and a flirting smile. I couldn't tell how old he was just by looking. I only hoped old enough.

He made an excuse to the gaggle of overweight women in hats and came over to me to ask me where I was headed. He was checking to see if we were waiting for the same delayed flight. I immediately smoothed my wrinkled clothes and told him that I was headed to New York. He was headed to California. He had been in the airport for an entire day already. I had been there for four hours and I had 10 to go.

I couldn't stop staring at Peter. His voice was the voice of a radio announcer. Strong but calming. "Who are all of those women?" I said smiling as I looked up at him.

"The one with the biggest purple hat is my Aunt Gladys. The rest of them are her sisters."

"How many sisters does she have?"

"They're not her real sisters, they are her church sisters. They're on a traveling revival. They had an extra ticket and I volunteered to go to help with their luggage. There's no telling what a bunch of traveling church sisters can do to get themselves into trouble!"

"That sounds like a nightmare," I said, regretting it as soon as it fell out of my mouth.

"The family who prays together stays together," is what Peter said to me, smiling and rolling his eyes.

I couldn't tell if he was serious or not. I tried to untwist my empty smile that was morphing into a frown of disbelief, but Peter caught me and said, "I know that must sound a little weird. We've been through a lot. My Aunty in that big purple hat raised me. God has been especially powerful for us in the last couple of years after my uncle died in a crane accident."

I didn't want to tell him about Marigold and the subway. I was trying to be upbeat since that's the way you're supposed to be when you meet a tall gorgeous stranger. I said, "I'm so sorry to hear that you lost your uncle."

"I miss him and I know that Aunt Gladys misses him, but I know it must have been God's plan for us. He has a plan for all of us. I'm sure he planned *this*. What are the chances that you and I would meet in an airport of all places, if it weren't for God's plan?"

"What are the chances?" I asked, surprised to hear such virtuous words coming from a man's mouth. His innocence was seductive.

I was drawn into the deliciousness of Peter's full lips that I had been fantasizing about since I first saw him.

"So, what do you do?" his blue eyes stared right through me.

How did you get those eyes, I wanted to ask him, but I just answered the question. "I work in a recording studio."

"You do? That's interesting," he said.

"What's interesting about it?"

"Well, I'm a drummer."

"Are you in a band or are you a session player?"

"Neither. I'm in construction. That's what I do to keep the roof over our heads."

"You don't play anymore?"

"No. Life called and I had to make some hard choices. Give up my dream and all that stuff." He was shy about it. His demeanor changed.

The more we talked it was apparent that he was not like the guys from the music industry that I had known in New York. Peter wasn't competitive or even determined. He was just a simple man who loved the sound of a drum.

Peter was like a character from a book. He was too good to be true. But he was standing right in front of me. He was righteous, gorgeous, and had a sense of humor. He was gentle and strong. His generous lips looked heavenly. I had endured too many good times with bad boys. Peter had virtue. He felt like a promise being kept.

Spending the whole day with Peter changed me. He was living proof that there was another place to put my faith besides the towering CD cabinet that had become my altar. After mourning Marigold for over 15 years, I was ready to rescind my battle with God, if it meant that I could have a man like Peter. I was ready to forgive God's thievery, so shamelessly stealing Marigold right out from under me that Monday night on the subway. I was ready to swim in the warm water of Peter's love. A life with Peter could heal me. I could feel he was the turning point.

When I stepped off the plane in JFK after my interrupted annual spa getaway and a whole day with Peter Holmes, I was changed. Zachary Jones, the 50-year-old man that I had been dating was just where I told him to be; the first baggage carousel. He looked like a cartoon character with his extra-long stemmed rose, white linen get-up, and a cloud of expensive cologne coming towards my lips. He was smooth and wrinkled at the same time. He wore a half-carat diamond earring in each ear and tinted blue mirrored sunglasses. It had been his graying ponytail, smooth reddish complexion, and red convertible that had drawn me to him, but that was all before Peter Holmes. Standing at Baggage Claim, I was suddenly repulsed. Peter was someone "of substance," as Marigold used to say about people who were deeper than we were.

Zachary drove me home and his sports car roared. I didn't say much. I looked up at the stars and thought of my day with Peter Holmes. Zachary was lamenting in the background about how much he missed me. When we arrived at my apartment, I thanked him for the rose and then broke the news. "I hate to tell you this. Please don't be angry. But, I can't see you anymore."

He took his blue tinted shades off and said, "You were only gone for four days..."

As I walked around the car to get my bags out of his tiny trunk, I said simply, "What a difference a day makes." He cursed after me as the doorman opened the door for me and then closed it on smooth Zachary Jones.

After five months of incessant talking on the phone, five trips to Ladera, California and falling asleep together with the phone plastered to our ears, I asked Peter, "What should we do now?"

"Get married," is what he said without hesitation.

The "M" word was daunting. It was as if it were an ancient word that was no longer taught in schools. It was a word that Roy never taught or encouraged. I did love Peter. He was generous and consistent. He called when he said he would. He kept his word. He never lied to me. He loved and respected his Aunt and his cousins. Family and commitment came easily to him. I yearned for that.

"Morgan, you'll never guess what happened today," he said anxiously.

"What?" I asked from the center of the bed where I always sat when talking to Peter at the same time every evening. I had become accustomed to rushing home from the studio just to get his calls. My friends wondered what had come over me. I was the original lets-go-for-a-drink-after-work girl. But when I met Peter everything in me changed.

"I asked for a transfer to move to New York."

"You did?" I said.

"I want to be with you, my love," Peter said into the phone, causing me to shiver slightly. "I don't want to be apart any longer."

We both fell silent. I didn't want to be apart from him either, but I didn't think I was ready for him to be permanent so soon. He finally said, "I can be fully moved in the next few months."

I spoke slowly, trying to buy time for my spinning brain to come up with something. "Already having a job is half the battle," is all I could say.

"I told my boss that I needed to discuss it with my honey. So what do you say, honey?"

"It sounds exciting," I said nervously, sweat building up on my forehead.

Then, Peter snapped out of the dreamland that we had both wandered into and said, "I think we should both pray about all of this. This is a life-changing decision for both of us... I just have to pray about leaving Auntie G and my cousins. I'll need to fast."

"I love you, Peter. Do what you have to do. Take all the time you need," I said nervously. I feared it would be too long and not long enough.

New York City, 2003

"Y'all just got here! Ava, it's stupid for you to lie on the couch when your bed is waiting for you. Why are you so tired? Why don't you go get in the bed?" Roy had opened the louvered doors and my old twin bed from childhood was staring at me. It was sagging onto the pull-out trundle bed beneath it where my husband and daughter would sleep when the day was done. The bed sheets were unchanged since the last time I visited.

"You don't look good," Daddy mumbled, shaking his head as he left his slippers for Rain to play with. He walked with bare feet towards me to help me off the couch. I let him take my arm and guide me to my childhood bed.

Neither Peter nor Daddy knew that the day before I had a battery of blood tests done in Oro Valley. I also kept it to myself that my doctor would be calling with the results.

Dr. Valdez kept his promise. He called.

Without much fanfare, Dr. Valdez said, "Morgan, your blood results indicate that you have Lupus. The severe type: Systemic Lupus Erythematosus." After too much silence, he said, "I know you must be very shocked. Do you have any immediate questions for me?"

"What's it called again? Never heard of it. I can't even pronounce it." I was shaking.

Dr. Valdez said, "It's a treatable auto-immune disease, common among women of color. What it means is that it's going to be hard in the beginning but it's treatable. It will change your life simply because it's chronic. There's no cure but it'll get easier after the meds start to take effect."

"Is it related to AIDS?" was my first thought, remembering the careless string of boys that I had devoured in my lifetime. "Will I die? Meds? How many meds will I have to take?" My heart was beating fast and the butterflies in my stomach were fluttering so fast that I wished I could vomit to free them. All I could hear in my head was Roy saying, "Ava, how stupid."

"It's nothing like AIDS. Survival rates for Lupus patients are excellent. Morgan, there's lots to talk about when you get back to Arizona. Why don't we wait until then? And, bring your husband. Peter, isn't it? He'll need to be there, too. He'll be a very important part of helping you get through this. You won't be able to do it alone."

"That doesn't sound good. Can it even wait until next week?"

"Yes and no," Dr. Valdez said. "All I ask is that you stay in bed. I'll call in a prescription for you. It's just one pill that you'll need to take twice a day with meals. It's called Plaquenil. That should help the achiness in your joints that I'm sure you're feeling. It's the most common drug for Lupus patients. It's important that we get you started on it now. I'll see you when you get back. It'll be OK, Morgan. Just take care and rest. Any more questions?"

"No."

I got off the phone and didn't tell Daddy. I suspected that in Daddy's loss for words, he would reach for his familiar – blaming me. He would say that I got Lupus because, "I did too much," or "stayed out too late," "because I ate sushi," or because "you moved in and married the li'l drummer boy."

New York City and Ladera Heights, California 1993

After five days of praying and fasting, God came through. He told Peter that he could move to New York to live with me. We planned the move for the approaching January, after I would spend Christmas with the Holmes family in Ladera Heights. I didn't know how to act in front of so many religious God-fearing Baptists. I had tattoos all over my body and because of California's heat, even at Christmas, I'd have to wear sleeveless shirts. *I didn't want to go.*

Peter had told all of his friends about me, including all of the women from church that were begging for his attention. He had been so proud to announce that he had fallen in love. He had called Abigail, Davina, Teresa, Gabriella, and Shaquina to share his good news. They all wished him good luck, offered to pray for him and probably gossiped amongst themselves that it would never last.

The Holmes family was sort of like an optical illusion. There was Aunt Gladys, Peter, and two cousins in their late teens. They looked like a traditional family: a young handsome man, a much older woman in a large hat and two older teens. No one really belonged to anyone, but they were a family.

They lived in a cookie-cutter five bedroom house with a white picket fence and a three-car garage. Sunlight blasted through every floor-to-ceiling window in the house. The garage was full with two matching Fords with personalized vanity plates that were known all over town: "Holmes 1" and "Mrs. Holmes." Mrs. Holmes kept Mr. Holmes's car even after he had passed away. Peter had already warned me about the car, which had been moved from the construction site and brought home the day of the accident, and not moved since. He also told me about the unforgettable Bible display at the front door. Gladys had arranged all of the family's personalized leather bibles in a stack at the doorway, so that no one could ever say that they forgot their bibles on the way to church.

Christmas in Ladera Heights went as expected, except that Peter surprised me at the supermarket with a one carat diamond, asking me to marry him from one knee in the produce section. I was taken aback but taken by the moment and the crowd that had gathered. I said "Yes!" happily and with relief. *Most of the Eastside girls were already married.*

When we announced our engagement to Aunt Gladys, the cousins, and the next door neighbors, the wrinkles of strained joy were carved into all of their faces. While I was in the kitchen helping Gladys set the table, she said timidly, "Morgan, I really don't mean to be impolite, and it's just my humble opinion, but, I just don't think you and Peter have anything in common. You've already done so much..." she said, eyeing my tattoos. "Peter's still establishing himself. He didn't even finish college. You know he hasn't done anything yet. He has so much still to learn. Why would a woman like you *want* to marry someone so different from yourself? You two hail from completely different *worlds.* Trust me."

The gospel music playing in the living room was too loud. Both Gladys and I tried to be discrete and not louder than the choir. I whispered, "Because I love him. That's why."

"Love is not the only thing that makes a marriage last," she said as she dropped the knives in front of me on the counter with a clang.

Just as I felt the heat of the knives on my palm, she hissed, "Watch it. They're a little hot, fresh out of the dishwasher."

Luckily, I didn't have to stay with Gladys who still cried herself to sleep every night since Uncle Ezekiel died in 1991, according to Peter. Peter had his own house that he shared with his best friend from high school and their two huge Doberman Pinschers; Blood and Bullet. His roommate Greg was equally enthralled with me; the tattooed lady from New York. Greg had been shot by a gang's stray bullet soon after high school. He developed a terrible permanent limp, so Greg was enthralled at any woman that he encountered, since his days of having one of his own were pretty much gone before they started.

New York City, January 2, 1994

Arriving back in New York with Peter on my arm and a one carat diamond on my finger made me feel brand new. New York's air seemed fresher with a fiancé. I ignored Marigold's snobbish voice roaring in my head, warning me that a hand-me-down diamond that once belonged to a grandmother was not a good sign of future prosperity. I rationalized that she would have liked Peter, if she had only lived. Peter would have convinced her that he had great potential. Besides, Marigold had married Roy, who had some money but lots of other problems like black rage. Peter was a sweet, innocent man. He was just what I needed.

Roy worried obsessively about when Peter would start his job. Although Peter hadn't gotten a start date yet, he had already moved to New York. The problem with the start date, we learned, was with Peter's visa, which was delaying the process of his job transfer. I didn't know that Peter needed a visa. He hadn't wanted me to know but eventually had to tell me the whole story.

My story is that Peter didn't look Jamaican. The real story is that he was. His fair creamy complexion had me fooled. His lack of any detectable accent also allowed me to think he was American. The only clue was that he was a handsome man who was actually eager to get married. *I should have known then.*

We were laying in bed when Peter decided to tell me the story. "Morgan, you've waited long enough. I am going to tell you the whole story of why I live with my Aunt, why I don't know my mother and why the job thing never happened. But you must promise to never share it with anyone else. Especially not your father."

"I promise," I said, holding his hand, caressing it. *What could be so bad?*

"You want to know about my mother? She got involved in some bad stuff in Jamaica. She and her boyfriend, my father, I guess, couldn't get visas to come to the States."

"Still, after all of this time?"

"Yes. The United States is not as welcoming to strangers as they would have the world think. The man who fathered me was caught up in a ganja ring. He was making a lot of money which is what drew my mother to him. She wanted to come to America, too. He made all kinds of promises to her. She made a mistake by trusting him. He told her she only had to do one thing. But since she was naïve, she got caught doing it. Delroy was his name. He kept her under the radar for a while, but when it was time for them to apply for visas their names were all over St. Thomas parish as wanted."

"She never tried again to come or to find you?" I asked.

Peter kept a straight face. He was no longer emotional about this disturbing reality of his life, while I was tearing up just hearing of a child lost in the world and not being able to be with his mother. That's how I felt. *Only I was looking for her*.

"Don't cry about it. She did the right thing sending me to the US. There was nothing for me except for trouble in St. Thomas. My mother wanted me to have a better life than she had. She knew it would be better if Gladys raised me."

"How did Gladys end up in America?"

"She was trained as a nurse in Jamaica. She got sponsored and was able to come to America on a work visa. When she met Ezekiel he was able to complete her immigration process by getting married. Which is what I am asking you to do for me. I love you Morgan and I want to make you happy."

My head was spinning with all of this new information. Suddenly I felt dizzy with betrayal. I didn't understand how Peter could have left so much out when telling me his story. I loved the warmth of his touch and the sincerity in his eyes, but I no longer trusted him. I had nowhere to go. I could never tell Roy that Peter was Jamaican and he would use me to get his visa. I could never tell him any of it. I had to continue with the love story that I had created.

"Why didn't you want me to know that you were Jamaican?" was all I could ask.

"When I met your friends from Eastside I didn't want them to judge me and think that I wasn't good enough for you. Girls like that only think of one thing when they think of Jamaica; dreadlocks and ganja. I didn't want to ruin your reputation with them or my chance to impress them. I want them to see how much I love you."

"Don't you ever miss your mother?"

"Yes and no. I miss the idea of her but—"

"It's more than an idea. A mother is a part of your soul," I said feeling the pain of motherlessness.

Peter continued, "Not for everyone, Morgan. Perhaps just for you. I had a mother figure and that is better than a lot of people. Gladys has done everything for me. She is more like a grandmother than a mother, but I consider her a mother out of respect for her. She never could have children. We both filled a void in each other. I miss my mother's soft hands and her strong hugs. But I also can remember how idle everyone was in St. Thomas, the parish that I'm from. I remember all of the young boys who got into the ganja trade instead of going to school. All they wanted was money. They all started young. It was a dead end there. I'll never forget my mother whispering in my ear, "I'm gonna get you out of here. I promise." I remember those words the most. She loved me enough to let me go. She sent me to Gladys because Gladys had a good life in California. She was a professional. After 20 years of nursing, the job at the prison opened up and she has been in charge of the Clinical Services Department ever since."

When Aunt Gladys and Uncle Zeke informally adopted him as a four year old, they gave him their name and everything he ever wanted.

When he applied to college initially, he thought he didn't need proof of citizenship. When they started looking into his records, he was kicked out. He never told anyone why. He used music as the excuse. He toured around with local bands until the gigs stopped coming. When he started working with his Uncle Zeke, he managed to slip through again. Peter wouldn't have to worry about it again until he would marry. In his mind, that would be the last time.

The immigration process was long and grueling. We had to ask Pietra and Daniella to submit affidavits confirming that we were really in a relationship and in love. I had to write the longest statement, confirming that I loved Peter and he had come for love alone. Peter's statement was muddy because of his informal adoption and the reality of his Jamaican birth certificate. It almost didn't work, but someone from EGA had a connection at Immigration and was able to get Peter's paperwork through. We kept Peter's immigration status from Roy. Neither of us wanted to fuel his xenophobic fire. Peter never told me as much as he should have.

While we waited for Peter's green card and for his job to start, every Sunday Roy brought over *The New York Times*. Just the classified section. He would leave the rest of the newspaper on his kitchen table. Whenever I would leave the room to check on dinner or to go get something from the kitchen, Roy would follow after me, whispering in my ear, "I don't want him to use you. You barely know him. I don't want to leave my money to a stranger. He's gotta get a job and soon! Don't believe all that stuff he told you. He doesn't really have a job."

I didn't want to doubt Peter. I loved him, I just didn't trust him as much. Peter eventually found a job in the paper. He applied for a position as a manager/host for an upscale restaurant on the Upper East Side called The Lake. The owner had been impressed with the manners that Gladys taught him and his irresistible face that was a gift from the father that no one spoke of. Godfrey, the owner of The Lake promised that he would personally train Peter on the specifics of the position. He paid Peter a hefty under-the-table salary.

Roy would finally sleep, with one eye open.

New York City, September 1995

Peter and I were finally married at the Waldorf Astoria in New York City. Aunt Gladys came kicking and screaming in a tight red gown that was about two sizes too small. Roy wore a friendly scowl and a flawless navy blue Christian Dior tuxedo. I wore a beige strapless gown of which Roy disapproved. *White was just not appropriate.* The wedding was packed with Eastside girls and their husbands eager to meet Peter so they could witness an EGA girl choosing a man for the contents of his heart, not his wallet, as we had all been trained to do.

Aunt Gladys' family and friends were gracious but awkward. They were trying their hardest to understand Peter's new wife: an uppity New Yorker with peculiar food tastes. I had insisted on a raw seafood bar and nothing fried or breaded on the menu. The Eastside girls were delighted and satiated. The guests from California left the wedding desperate for a fast food restaurant and complaining about the raw fish.

At the altar, Roy had slapped my hand into Peter's and whispered, "Good luck! She's very expensive."

New York City, 1998

It took about three years when Peter started *wanting*. For Peter, the world was suddenly much bigger than the malls and chain restaurants of Ladera Heights or the mountains of Jamaica where he was born. His friends from The Lake came from places like India, Belgium, and Spain. They all had accents, strange customs and exotic foods that Peter had never experienced. His new friends started inviting him out to smoke $12 cigars, play pool in downtown pool halls, and go to off-Broadway plays. One of them was even gay. Peter's world had suddenly grown and he no longer wanted to be so small.

Peter's boss was constantly taking the entire management staff to other upscale restaurants around the city to see what the competition was doing. He ordered hundred-dollar bottles of wine for them to sample while they analyzed the restaurant's service. When he wasn't working, Peter's daily uniform became cashmere cardigans from Brooks Brothers and shoes from L.L.Bean. When Peter was dressed in his prep school finery, the Eastside Girls almost couldn't tell him apart from someone they would have, maybe, *dated*. They reluctantly approved of him because he made me happy. I ignored the inkling to worry about the things I didn't know.

The year before the wanting, Peter announced as I was crawling into bed after a late night at the studio, "I'm going to finish my degree in music education and land a job at one of those private schools in New York. You have connections, because you went to Eastside, right?"

My head had already hit the pillow. To quiet him I said, "Some. Maybe someone we know can get you a job interview at least. But that's years away. You have to finish first."

He wanted to talk more. "I need to do it, Morgan. The people in New York are so *different*. I want a respectable career. Now that we're married, I'm legitimate. I don't want to be a glorified waiter forever. All of the guys at work are working toward careers. I want to make you and your father proud."

By the time Peter started night school, we had become roommates. We had adopted the fast-paced negligent life of married New Yorkers. Our dinners consisted of leftover Chinese or take-out Dominican food. Only our answering machine message indicated that we shared a tiny New York space that we called a home. The seasons flew by carelessly with only the purchases of new boots and jackets as proof that time was passing. We were drifting further and further apart, only seemingly connected on holidays when we were forced to pretend in front of Aunt Gladys, her neighbors, or Roy. Peter had fallen deeply in love with the wonders and promises of New York and I had tired of it.

When we were at home, the walls felt tight around us. Peter complained, "It's not proper for a woman to be out so late at night working. That's what a man's supposed to do."

"Who are all those strangers calling our house so late?" I yelled back.

"Linen closets are for linens, not shoes!" Peter would say.

I remember the exact day in 1998 that I took flight from New York City. I was on the subway, going to a meeting. A black girl who couldn't have been older than 18 was strolling her baby on the platform. In his rush, a graying white man accidentally bumped into her stroller. The girl exploded, "Motherfucka watch where you goin'. Shit!"

The black girl's baby stared blankly onto the train track, as if she had heard such clatter every day of her life. The white man reddened and apologized profusely. She couldn't hear him over the cacophony of her insults and obscenities. The more he pleaded, "I'm sorry," the louder she was.

The lights and the clatter of the #2 Southbound train muted her rant. When I finally stepped inside the air conditioned train car, I found a seat. Tears spilled from my eyes. I started to shiver, remembering that this hard gray seat on the #2 train was Marigold's deathbed. As the train pulled out of the station, I could still see the girl ranting and raving while the white man stood, shrinking.

Voices pounded in my head. *You need to go. Life here can't go on. Especially, if you want a family.* Like Marigold, I had a vision of what my life should look like and I was determined to see it... *I could almost taste it.*

I told Peter that I wanted out of New York at a Cuban restaurant called Black Beans. "I feel trapped in New York," I started. "I think we should start talking about moving. Maybe we should go back West. It's getting too hard here and you've been in New York for close to five years. You could be closer to Aunt Gladys."

"How trapped could you feel? We live in a luxury condo on Riverside Drive with two bathrooms and a doorman? Peter said, raising his voice to compete with the din in the restaurant.

I could barely hear what he was saying.

"Is everything OK here?" the waitress interrupted.

"It's fine. Thank you," I said, slightly annoyed.

The huge man at the table closest to us was trying to squeeze out of the tight space between us. As he started to leave for the bathroom, his napkin fell to the floor and he bumped my chair trying to get it. My glass of red wine slapped my leg like blood, frazzling me. I wanted to explode like that girl on the subway, but I knew Peter couldn't stand the site of rage. I held my anger in and signaled with my hand that it was OK. The man looked embarrassed and quickly headed to the bathroom.

The smell of the red wine penetrated my clothing and my nostrils. I had the desperate need to shower but was distracted by straining to hear Peter "…A great job at The Lake. My boss…promote me…"

"Peter, what's more important? Money or family?"

"I'm *trying* to do what's right for us. I am the man of the house. That's why I went back to school. I want to be able to tell our child someday that I also graduated from college. You can't be the only one with a degree."

"I don't think I can wait anymore. I need to get out of here."

"I considered going back to school when I first got here, but your father wouldn't let up on me about finding a job while I was waiting for my job to start."

"Thank God he was on you. He was right, the job that you came for never started."

Peter looked down.

Peter got up, paid the bill and came back to the table and extended his hand.

As we stepped out onto Amsterdam Avenue, I eyed the graffiti all around me and the dirty streets. "Let me tell you what happened to me today." I proceeded to tell him about the black girl with her fingernails curled into claws and her fake candy-apple-red weave that covered one eye. I told him about the ugly words she used in front of her child and the hateful words she called a perfect stranger…and how ashamed I felt to be a New Yorker. "I hate it here. I've got to get out," I sputtered.

"I'm sorry all that happened to you, Morgan, but it's got nothing to do with us. We will get out of here, someday. There's no rush. We have a whole life ahead of us. All you need to do is pray for peace inside yourself."

New York City, 2003

Peter and Rain had already gone back home to Oro Valley. Peter had to get back to work. He had recently become a manager at Red Lobster. They had been impressed with his resume from The Lake. Rain went back to daycare, since I was not feeling well enough to keep her with me. My boss in Oro Valley had thought it would be a good idea for me to do some networking in New York, so they had given me a couple of extra days of vacation. My boss was determined to get some New York accounts for the state-of-the-art studio that was nestled in the Tortolita Mountains. When I called my boss to tell him about the call from Dr. Valdez, he was audibly disappointed about my not being able to network but feigned proper concern. He sighed. I reassured him I would be back at work in no time and that I would come back to New York another time to make contacts. We both were lying.

A day after the call from Dr. Valdez, I stayed in bed all day. Roy felt sorry for me but all he knew was that I was "tired." He allowed me to stay in his bed while he slept in the living room on the lumpy couch that was once new and sleek and Marigold's taste. He mumbled under his breath about the Jews taking advantage of me. I let him.

I spent all of my days in New York eating very little, sleeping, and making excuses. I cancelled all of my lunch dates with the Eastside girls and with my closest music business friend, Dorian, who happened to be in New York for a job interview. I lied to them all because I wasn't ready to tell myself or any of my friends that I was sick.

"Ava, why don't you get up?" Roy would yell from the kitchen, trying to wake me while noon was approaching. "Do you want something to eat?"

"Daddy, if I wanted something to eat, wouldn't I have asked for it?"

"Little girl, don't talk to me like that. I'll get my strap." I noticed his gnarled knuckles had gotten worse since the year before. From the bed I saw that the belt still hung on the back of his bedroom door, swinging only when he slammed the door.

"I'm too old for the strap now. I'm a married woman."

"You're never too old when you're disrespecting ME. I mean it, Ava. I've had it with you talkin' to me like that. You've been pissy ever since you got here. I don't need this. You can take your ass back to Arizona, now, if you want. I'll drive you to the airport."

"Sorry, Daddy," I said as I turned over in his bed. I could feel my body rapidly failing me and I couldn't control my descent. I was like a plane crashing.

There were small white sores forming inside my mouth. I had awakened gagging with a desert-dry mouth and no appetite.

"Ava, what is *wrong* with you? Are you sick? You're acting so nasty and I know I haven't done anything to you. I've been damn nice to you. What's the matter with you, besides being so skinny? Maybe that's your problem. You're hungry! You need to e-a-t."

"I'm just tired, Daddy. I've been doing two jobs at work, managing the studio and booking the sessions and dealing with Rain. Until they find a replacement for me in Bookings, I have to do both jobs."

"Don't let those Jews kill you, Ava! They always want something for free. You can't do two jobs without two paychecks! Remember that. Take time out for y-o-u."

In the later 70's Marigold had adorned all the walls in the master bedroom with floor to ceiling mirrors. Roy left them as they were, as if he were expecting her, still. Turning to face the mirrors in front of the bed, I could see every affliction that was sprouting on my face. I could see how my eyeballs had swollen and seemed too big for my sockets. I tried to piece together some cohesive thoughts about how weak I felt and I couldn't string together one. If I moved too quickly, I was certain that my thoughts would fall out of my ears. I was trying desperately to hold on to what I was made of.

Roy woke me up the next morning yelling, "Ya better get up, Ava, if you want to go." Every year, Daddy would take me to Henri Bendel and Bergdorf Goodman to shop for things that Peter and I couldn't afford. It was raining outside and my knees felt ninety years old as I dragged myself out of his bed. Usually, I craved these days with Roy when I could be the indulged little girl that Marigold wanted me to be. Instead, I spent those tender years which should have been easy, raging against death. These shopping trips with Daddy made me feel that he and I had forgiven each other and Marigold for leaving us alone.

Roy had turned seventy eight that year. When we got off the Fifth Avenue bus at 57th street, he hopped down from the high step and spryly started toward the store. When he looked back I was still hanging on for dear life to the bus' handrail. He looked back and yelled, "Ava come on. We don't have all day. I have things I want to do!"

I couldn't come.

"What's wrong with you?" Daddy pleaded.

Once I caught up, we slowly walked into Bergdorf Goodman and the smell turned me inside out. My head spun not knowing where to look. I was dizzied by the skeletal figures that were prancing in front of my face, squirting the newest noxious perfume at me. I chose the down escalator to the perfume department because it was close. I walked to the closest counter, sprayed a shot of a fragrance that smelled like lemony urine into the air. I told the woman behind the glass case with a jet-black bob, ghostly complexion, and loud red lips to bag it up. I heard Roy sigh when the woman said, "That'll be $95.00 plus tax." Roy pulled out his fading pale green American Express Card and sucked his teeth.

"This is the last time I'm gonna do these trips. They cost me a fortune," he teased lightly with a heavy-hand. "Where to now?"

"Home."

"What?" Roy grunted.

"Daddy, let's go home. Thanks for the perfume. I'm tired now. Can we take a cab?"

"I thought you said you needed new jeans?"

"I need a cab."

"A cab? You know how much that'll cost?" Let's take the bus. You waste too much money. I'm not gonna leave you anything when I die, because you'll have it all spent up, before my body's even cold."

My eyes pleaded to get through the fog of air pollution, expensive perfume, and the smoke and mirrors of the Upper East Side. I desperately needed to get off my heavy legs. I didn't want to faint on 57th street, which would have been my fate, if I had to wait another minute for public transportation. *The #2 train took her.*

Roy mumbled under his breath about his Will until I couldn't hear him anymore. Tears started to spill from my swollen eyes. He said nothing but asked me to hold the tiny lavender shopping bag while he hailed a cab. The bag was too heavy.

"Being a black man in New York can be a liability out here," he complained. "These foreigners!" he said referring to all cab drivers. Finally, one slowed in front of us.

Inside the cab, Roy looked out of the window and away from me. The thick odious smell of the Jamaican driver was like a third passenger. I cleared my throat to try to keep the pungent aroma out of my vulnerable body. My father was trying to get the window down, but it was stuck. Daddy turned to me and whispered into my ear, "What's that smell?"

I whispered, "I don't know," smelling only his hot dry breath burning my eardrum.

"It's *him*," Daddy hissed, eyeing the back of the driver's head which was stacked high with thick sinewy dreadlocks. "Peee-yooo!" he whispered holding his nose, reminding me of the high-pitched sound he used to make when I was a little girl. *He could never know about Peter.*

I looked out the window and saw that the afternoon traffic in midtown was thick. Car horns blared continuously. New Yorkers were frantically running from one place to the next, dodging cars and each other. They held on to their cell phones as if they were life.

Daddy turned serious. "Ava, I'm gonna ask you one more time, what's wrong with you?" His voice was tender, it was the Daddy voice. The voice that melted me.

"Daddy, I'm sick."

"Sick with what?"

"The Doctor says I have Lupus."

"Lupus? How'd you get that? Is that AIDS?"

"No. It's an auto-immune disease. I don't know anything more about it, but I have it. All I know is that I feel so weak. I'm swelling in places that I didn't know I had."

"Is that why you're so skinny? And your eyes so swollen?"

"I'm scared, Daddy."

"I know, darlin'. It wouldn't be life if it wasn't scary."

When we got home, I headed straight for Daddy's bedroom to put my pajamas on. It was still broad daylight. The secrets of my body were seeping out.

I heard my father in the kitchen making a cup of the instant coffee that always made his mouth dry and his breath rancid. I knew he would go to the dining room table and talk it over with himself. My stomach churned thinking of the smell of the coffee on his dry diabetic tongue. I could hear him groping to understand. I heard him, "Lupus? What *is* Lupus?" "Lupus? How'd she get it?" "Lupus, my baby has *Lupus*. She's been through enough. We can't take no more. How could this happen?"

I closed my eyes. I had no idea.

CHAPTER 4 | *Chaos*

Oro Valley, Arizona 1999

We were visiting Aunt Gladys from New York when Pastor Jackson came to dinner to see us. He recommended that we visit Oro Valley, Arizona someday. "It's an up and coming city. Full of young families," he had said twirling a frayed toothpick into a crevice of a molar. "I read about it in *Pastor Today* Magazine. They have lots of great churches, too."

I convinced Peter that we should check it out for our next vacation. He agreed. As soon as we stepped into the airport the next summer, we were met with the warm aroma of baking sand. As we drove through the desert streets with the top down of our rented convertible, I marveled, "Look at these houses, Babe!" Oro Valley's landscape was dramatic, unfamiliar and exactly what I needed. It was unpretentious, no one dressed up and the houses were made of earth.

It was a perfect place for me to finally lay my New York burden down.

"Yeah. They're cool," is all Peter said.

I pushed, "Wouldn't you like to live in a house like this someday?"

"Maybe...but not anytime soon," he said scoping out the streets for authentic Mexican Restaurants.

"When do you think?" I asked the back of his head.

"I don't know. Maybe in about five more years," he responded, not looking at me.

"Something like that," I said. *Yeah right*. I thought.

I was ready, already. Peter didn't know how desperately I needed to get out of New York. I was on the run trying to get away from bad memories. I just couldn't get that black girl or the subway out of my head.

Resentment is a sly animal. It skulks around without any scent and once it is upon you – suddenly everything reeks. Resentment shows itself in so many ways. It is like invisible ink. You can almost see it at first but only after it has dried; it leaves a subtly ugly smudge.

When we got back to New York from our desert vacation, everything was the same except for me. I was no longer obsessed with working at the studio. Peter was coming home later and later because he was busy with school and his new friends, which afforded me more time alone to dream my desert dreams and search online for our future. I knew Peter would move. He would have to.

Peter didn't want to move.

I did.

He didn't.

I insisted.

We moved.

I thought I had won.

I had won…and lost Peter at the same time.

New York City, LaGuardia Airport 2003

Daddy held me tightly and buried his head in my neck with the same hard grief that he did the night that Marigold died. Daddy was crying as he stood next to Dorian, who had insisted that he go with Daddy and me to the airport. I had finally told Dorian why I cancelled lunch. When I revealed the truth of my failing body, he barged right in, insisting that he see me face-to-face and help by accompanying us to the airport.

Daddy had always liked Dorian. He had graduated from college and was already successful in the music business, running a large recording studio in Atlanta and working part time as a tour manager for some smaller acts on the side. At that time he happened to be in New York for a job interview at a larger studio. As Dorian took my bags and loaded them into the cab, my father looked at Dorian with a tangled look of regret. Daddy and I rode to the airport in silence, while Dorian tried desperately to make conversation. Daddy and I were both lost in our thoughts about what was to come, while Dorian's questions and comments were left suspended in mid-air.

When we arrived at the airport, as Dorian helped me out of the cab, I said, "Thank you for coming. Sorry I'm not in a great mood. After I see the doctor, I'll let you know what he says."

Dorian rubbed my back with his oversized hand and said, "Anytime, Morgan. We were both here at the same time and I had to see you. I'm so sorry to hear about your health, but you'll get better. Let me know how I can help. I'll be back in Atlanta at the end of the week. I'll call you. Don't worry about your Dad. I'll get him back home safely."

"Be careful, he's not in a great mood today."

"He loves me. It's you that pisses him off," Dorian whispered.

Daddy broke his silence, "Don't miss your plane talkin' so much. Ya better get goin'. I'm sorry I get so mad at ya, baby. But you're my only baby and I worry about ya."

"That's OK. Daddy. I'm sorry I was so rude."

"I understand. Being sick can make ya sick," he said with tears in his eyes.

"Bye Daddy," I said loosening his grip.

He corrected me, tugging my arm to keep me close, "Don't say, 'Goodbye.' Just say, 'until the next time.'"

As I sat on the plane, waiting for takeoff, I couldn't get Peter's limp reaction to my news out of my mind. "Peter, I have something to tell you," I started. "Dr. Valdez called to tell me that I have Lupus. Systemic Lupus Erythematosus."

Peter's silence seemed to have lasted forever when he finally said, "Morgan, the Lord has been good to us. He would never forsake us. This is just a test of our faith. Just hold on to God's unchanging hand."

What does that mean? I wanted to say, but I knew that he probably didn't know either.

In that moment of crisis, I yearned for him to say something I could believe in. Something original, something that would matter to *me.* I longed for, "I'll stick by you through this. You can always depend on me."

New York City, 1996

Aunt Gladys had advised that I should allow Peter to be the spiritual leader of our household. So, we joined God's Love Baptist

Church in Harlem. Gladys also advised that I should be baptized to give the beginning of our spiritual life together the newness that it deserved.

The week before the baptism, the church had sent a long letter detailing what I needed to bring for "Baptism Sunday." The list read:

A change of underwear

Something to wrap my head

A new toothbrush and toothpaste

The church will provide you with a safe place for your belongings and a baptism robe.

Since religion was Peter's specialty, I asked him to explain what the new toothbrush was for. He explained, "It's symbolic. You will be cleaning your mouth out after all of the unclean things you said and did with it, before you become saved. It's a new beginning."

I could hear Marigold in my head, *Ridiculous.*

I said to my husband, "Oh. That makes sense."

When the pastor put my head under the water, my brain swirled around the murky waters of the Christian's conundrum. As the pastor immersed me into the tepid water, visions and fears came up. Was this holy water powerful enough to convince me that a woman who had been violently raped didn't deserve the right to heal and choose life for herself instead of carrying a life that was forced upon her? Would this holy water morph me into a talking head for fear, and hatred? Would this water cleanse my eyes so much that they would no longer see what was obvious? Would I come up from this water no longer able to detect that Brother Amos, the minister of music may have a boyfriend, not a wife? Would these waters turn me blind, deaf and dumb? As the Pastor brought me up from the water, I shuddered and shook.

He whispered into my ear, "Sister, you are born again."

No. I'm not. Thank God.

But I had just drowned in shallow waters.

Roy, Peter, and I celebrated my baptism with a brunch of fried catfish, grits, and cheap mimosas at a breakfast dive in Harlem called Pan Pan. I was expected to call Gladys as soon as I got home to tell her that I received my tithing envelopes and that I was going to start using them right away. In private, Roy and I had always laughed at the insanity of giving away 10% of my earnings.

But over catfish and grits and in front of Peter, Roy toasted, "Now I can go to my grave. You are protected by God's love. Ava, you are finally, saved."

Peter and Roy high-fived over my head while Peter said, "Praise the Lord!"

Roy said, "It's about time."

Roy's "Christianity" was very different from Gladys and Ezekiel. Daddy went to church "when he felt like it" and Marigold never went at all. Marigold thought that black Baptists were "zealots, hypocrites, and not to be trusted." As a Christian Scientist she didn't have to do anything, go anywhere and she could believe whatever she wanted. She liked it that way.

Roy was torn. He knew of the lack of rational thinking that came with being a Christian but knew that going to church tethered him to black people and he wanted that for both of us. Marigold always seemed more interested in befriending people that thought like her. Black people never really liked her because she dared to question too many things. Roy had wisely mastered Christian rhetoric. In his spare time he would peek into the whisper thin pages of the Bible, memorize the most commonly used verses and clichés and spout them at all the right moments.

How are you, today Miss Berniece?

Too blessed to be stressed, Brother Blackmon.

Alright then. You go on with your bad self, Sister.

Christians were sold on Roy. He never let on that his true religion was rage.

On the weekends, I remember Roy watching Gil Noble's program, *Like it Is*. He would watch it with popcorn and a cup of instant coffee in the mornings. He would get so excited, yelling at the black-and-white screen when Jesse Jackson or Dick Gregory were guests. "You said it, Jesse! Dick, we can't let 'em hold us down no more! Ava, you don't know nothin' about this!"

I was afraid to.

Oro Valley, Arizona 2003

I woke up startled. A flight attendant was shaking me. "It is time to deplane, Miss. We have landed in Arizona. You are the last person on the plane."

It took me a minute to re-group. The Plaquenil insert had mentioned that dizziness was a side effect. I gathered my things, slowly, and deplaned, dreading everything that was to come. As soon as I stepped into the airport, I was enveloped by the familiar sweet smell of the desert's perfume.

As I clumsily approached Peter and Rain at the black velvet rope, Peter said, "Hi. Welcome home."

"Hi Peter," I said as I playfully pulled the bill of his baseball cap, like I used to when our love was alive. Rain reached out for me. She was wearing a tiny dark blue baseball cap, just like Peter's. I turned to Rain and said, "Hi sweet thing, did you miss Mommy?"

"We both did," Peter said, woefully. "You hungry?"

"Not really," I said as I dropped my bag and pulled Rain toward me. She was drooling on my shoulder and bouncing up and down. She weighed a ton. I started walking toward baggage claim, and Peter looked at my bag sitting there and decided not to make a fuss. He picked it up.

"Your lip is swollen. I read about that. You're limping. Your knee must be bothering you, too. It's just like how the website described it. I looked Lupus up."

"You went to a website? Did your website tell you about the little white sores that feel like bugs crawling inside my mouth? Did your website tell you how my lips constantly swell without warning?" I stopped walking because Rain had become too heavy for me. I handed her back to Peter. Rain's eyes filled with tears at the rejection.

He took her without saying anything. I limped while he walked, toting Rain and dragging my overstuffed bag.

"What causes all of that?" Peter said.

"Lupus," I said impatiently. "Can you come with me to the doctor tomorrow?"

The shrieks of joy around the airport made me feel woozy.

"You look great!"

"I'm so happy to see you!"

"How was your flight?"

"Welcome home!"

Other people's joy was loud and obnoxious as it ricocheted off the airport walls. The sound of other people's families filled me with sorrow. My own family was limping, quiet, and without an appetite. The booming loudspeaker barked flight status details and the names of lost parties looking to be found.

Peter said something that I didn't hear. "What'd you say?"

"I don't know if I can go to the doctor with you tomorrow. That's not a lot of notice. I took off today to pick you up."

"Did you tell your boss that I'm sick?"

"No. not yet."

"Why not? You have to tell him."

"I'll tell him when I need to."

"You need to, now. Doctor Valdez said that you have to be at the first appointment."

"I'll call my boss." He handed Rain back to me. I let her drool on my shirt while the bag sat on my ankle like a weight. Rain was falling asleep. Dizziness held me up.

Peter pulled out his cell phone and walked away.

"Tell him," I mouthed.

"I will," Peter mouthed back, as he walked further and further away.

Peter's boss allowed him to go to my appointment with Dr. Valdez. We dropped Rain off at daycare first thing the next morning and we were silent on the way to Dr. Valdez's office for my 8:30 appointment.

I nudged my way into the silence. "I'm scared, Peter."

"Morgan, I'm scared too. I don't know how to handle all of this. The website said that some people with Lupus live nearly normal lives. My Aunt and I prayed on the phone for over an hour after you called."

"That's good to know." *Did you fast?* I wanted to ask, but held my tongue.

Peter held my elbow as we made our way into the doctor's office. The temperature outside had already reached 99 degrees. We sat in the waiting room like two mummies wrapped in fear. We didn't look at each other but breathed in unison until we heard, "Morgan Holmes."

We were finally seated in Dr. Valdez's office. We sat in handmade high-backed leather chairs with embossed desert scenes adorning the backs of them. Peter caressed my cold hand. His touch was unfamiliar. We didn't know what to do with ourselves so we just stared at the wall behind Dr. Valdez's leather and wood desk.

"Good to see you, Morgan," Dr. Valdez said as he came into the room. "How're you feeling?" He turned to Peter and said, "You must be Peter, Morgan's husband?"

"That's me," Peter said, smiling like he was at a party trying to impress the host by being with the guest of honor. Peter jumped right in. "Doctor, it's not that bad is it?"

Dr. Valdez started slowly but the more words he spoke, the less I understood. He started, "Auto-immune diseases are just... background noise. Morgan can lead...somewhat...life, but she just has to...aware of certain things...in the background. The meds will... symptoms and...constantly monitor her.... As long...take your meds, she should be fine..."

My ear drums started to close as he read from the sheet divulging the results of my blood work. Certain words sounded familiar.

"Hemoglobin...Hermatocrit...Double stranded DNA...Urine..."

What does it all mean?

"Why is it called Lupus?" Peter interrupted.

Dr. Valdez said, "The term 'lupus' which is actually the Latin word for 'wolf', describes the rash that some people with Lupus get. It's called a Malar Rash. The rash goes across the face and it is sort of looks like the scar of a wolf bite."

"That will happen to my face?"

"Perhaps not. Everyone with Lupus doesn't get the rash."

My stomach started to flutter. I could feel tears starting again. Peter put his arm around me to comfort me.

Like a wolf, I wanted to howl.

"She'll get better won't she?" Peter asked.

"She should with the medications. I know it all sounds pretty bad, Morgan. I have several lupus patients. They're all doing just fine now."

"What did you say about her urine?" Peter asked.

"Urine?…Urine……Oh – Morgan has blood in her urine. Is that what you're referring to?" Dr. Valdez said.

Peter said, "What does that mean?"
Dr. Valdez face suddenly went grave. "It means she'll need to see a kidney specialist."

"A kidney specialist? For what?" I asked.

"Because there's evidence of blood in your urine…"

I was going deaf. The words seemed quieter and quieter. I couldn't comprehend a thing.

"One last question, Dr. Valdez. Why when I told my father about this, he asked me if this was related to AIDS?"

"Lupus is actually the opposite of AIDS. With AIDS, the patient has a non-existent immune system and with Lupus, you have an overactive immune system. If I can give you a visual…do you like dogs?"

"Not really," Peter and I said in unison.

"Try to imagine it, anyway…Lupus is like an overeager Golden Retriever running around inside your body licking, touching, and nipping at everything in sight, not caring which cells are good or bad. Lupus just wants to be loved. It is like a dog constantly saying, please pay attention to me."

"Can we shoot the dog?" I asked as I eyed a picture of Dr. Valdez and his Golden Retriever on his desk.

Smiling, Dr. Valdez said, "You can't shoot it. But you can calm it down with some good meds."

Dr. Tron was the nephrologist Dr. Valdez sent me to. He couldn't have been more than 35 years old. He was Asian, which according to Roy made him a "good doctor." He appeared studious, serious, and he spoke with an eerie whisper. The morning of the appointment with Dr. Tron, I was alone. I had woken up with transparent sores all over my face, lips, and hands. I had swollen knuckles and ankles. I could barely move down the corridors of Dr. Tron's vast office that he shared with five other nephrologists. It felt as though there was a bag of sand in my veins weighing down my blood and slowing everything down. The waiting room was full of senior citizens. I was embarrassed to be among them. I could feel their pity hitting me like spitballs.

Attached to a clipboard were my blood results. Dr. Tron read from the clip board which held his gaze. "Your disease is so active. I have never seen a case like this…with so many symptoms." Those were the words coming from his mouth, but all I could hear was *"You're dying."*

"I am going to order a rush kidney biopsy," he said, finally raising his head from the clipboard.

"What's that?"

Dr. Tron's back was to me as he said, "I'm going to inject your kidney with a needle and take out some tissue, so I can determine which drug to treat you with based on the condition of your kidneys.

I prayed while I waited for the anesthesia to work.

I woke up to Dr. Tron saying, "See, that wasn't so bad. We spoke to Peter and he's coming."

When Peter arrived, he was agitated. He greeted me with, "I'm going to get docked this time."

"What kind of thing is that to say to me after a kidney biopsy?"

"I'm scared of losing you. I don't want you to die. I can't raise Rain by myself. You can't die. You're too young. I can't talk about this anymore."

"Good news," Dr. Tron said when he called me with the biopsy results the next day. I had hobbled to the phone and Rain had followed close behind my slow heels.

"There's nothing wrong with my kidneys?" I said, hopefully.

"Not quite that good. But you only have mild irritation and I think I can treat it aggressively with Cellcept, the hottest drug out on the market that everyone is having great success with."

"Hot new drug on the market?" I repeated, disgusted by the commercialism of it all.

"I'll call in the prescription and you should be able to start taking it this afternoon. Take 1000 milligrams in the morning and 1000 in the evening. That should work until your next visit."

I looked down at Rain who was looking up at me. Tears fell from my eyes. I felt regret that Rain had been born. Neither she nor I were getting what we came here for. I looked at Rain's innocent gaze and her rosy brown cheeks and I wanted to run far away from this mess that Peter and I had made.

I opened my mouth as wide as I could and bellowed like the volume would take me away. Rain was startled at first, but then she smiled her inimitable toothless grin. Then she caught on to what she thought was a new game. She reached for me to no avail. I could no longer lift her. Rain screamed in response. She screamed and then I screamed louder. Luckily, we were isolated on our two acres. If someone had heard us, they would have thought a crime was being committed. *There was.*

After five minutes, I screamed a little quieter and she did too. Rain was still reaching for me as the screaming game came to a natural close. I sank down on the cold tile floor to be next to her.

Over the next week, my left knee grew to the size of a grapefruit. I hobbled around the house occasionally catching glimpses of myself in mirrors as an invalid. It was as if I was watching a movie; something tragic and not connected to me. When I grasped that it was me, my soul shriveled.

I tried calling Dr. Valdez and spoke to a nurse for some advice about my grapefruit-sized knee. The nurse called back saying, "The Doctor suggests Advil for the swelling."

After 6 tries, two tablets each try, the Advil didn't work.

When I called again, the nurse took a message and then called back saying, "Dr. Valdez suggests ice packs."

Ice didn't work.

The next day, I made an appointment. Peter couldn't get any more time off from work. I had managed to drive myself in complete silence. I could no longer listen to music and concentrate on driving at the same time. The sound of music took too much of what was left of me.

When Dr. Valdez took one look at my knee, he decided that it should be drained. He proceeded to take two syringes of a yellow piss-colored fluid out of my knee with a long evil needle. He gave me a shot of a liquid steroid to ease the pain and said he would call me if there was anything abnormal. "I'm sure there won't be," he assured me as he whisked out of the exam room.

But there was.

I had contracted Valley Fever, a fungus of the desert.

Dr. Valdez called me with the newest diagnosis and a request for more blood to be drawn. He also called with two new doctors for me to see. He recommended Dr. Garvey, a knee specialist, and Dr. Liverwood, an infectious disease doctor.

My care plan had gone from simple to complex. Plaquenil at first and within six weeks my requirements blossomed to Prednisone, Cellcept, Advil, Diflucan, ice packs, steroidal ointment, a cane, and a handicap sticker for my car. I thought about Marigold constantly. Wanting to be where she was. *Jealous that she hadn't had to go through all of this.*

Every time I left the pharmacy with a new prescription, I felt more and more tangled up inside. I was enraged at the carelessness of doctors and their perfunctory 10 minute drive-by appointments. I walked humbly to my car with a new awkward gait, a graying complexion, and a ghostly presence.

PART TWO

Soul Mining

CHAPTER 5 | *Crumbling*

Oro Valley, Arizona Fall 2004

Without any notice, the local chapter of the Healthy Women's Club must have rescinded my lifetime membership. They were polite about it. Instead of leaving me with no friends, they enthusiastically pushed for my membership into the *National* Chapter of the Unhealthy Women's Club. It seems that when healthy women hear of a friend's sickness, in order to fill the silence of regret, they resort to referring you to other random sick people from all over the country to replace themselves in your life. It is the Healthy Women's assumption that a community filled with ailing women will serve us much better than they could.

Once the Healthy Girls in my life had replaced themselves, they felt no remorse. Their calls and concern evaporated like rain in the desert. I understood. The Healthy Women obviously no longer had any use for me. I was no longer like them; a former New York City girl preoccupied with work and climbing corporate ladders. I could no longer afford indulgent trips to the spa and time-sucking appointments to get my hair and nails done. My life was no longer my own. My heart and soul belonged to Lupus and those whom Lupus chose. I call us Lupians, because we are aliens who skulk around with only glimpses of visible ills: red cheeks, swollen ankles, rashes... things that are easily mistaken for everyday discomforts. Truth is, Lupians ache mostly on the inside.

It was the constant chortling of the home phone and cell phone that comforted me when Lupus and I had run out of things to talk about, when we were alone and it seemed that all I could hear were echoes from my past. The phone calls from fellow Lupians usually included brief introductions telling me which of my former friends referred them, followed by comparisons of our physical malaise – mainly stiffness and swelling. Then they would offer me recipes for success or shower me with forewarnings of how to avoid the always pending "flare."

The day Rene Harden called for the first time, I was crumpled into my usual position on the worn brown leather couch, where the fine leather pressed into my cheek leaving a deep scar of perpetual lethargy. The TV was rambling in the background. I had started watching soap operas since I could watch them with half a gaze, and still keep up with the story lines.

I answered the phone groggily, reaching for the remote to turn down the shrieks on the TV between a woman and her husband who had cheated on her with their babysitter.

"Morgan Holmes, please."

"This is Morgan."

"This is Rene Harden from Los Angeles. Hope this is not a bad time. Beauregard Pettit from New York recommended that I call you. I heard about your recent diagnosis. I have Lupus, too."

I sat up, grateful for contact. "No, no. This is a good time," I said feeling the comfort of the black chenille blanket that I was buried under.

"How are you feeling, today?" Rene asked.

"I'm fine..." Then, I caught myself. This was a *Lupian*. "I'm fine as I can be under the circumstances." It was hard to give up dutiful pleasantry.

"What's going on today?" Rene probed.

"I'm exhausted. My ankles are swollen, my eyelids are puffy. I look drawn and worn out and I feel even worse. How's that?" I sat up, annoyance strengthening me.

"Sounds like a person with Lupus. How long have you been on your medication?"

"A couple of months. Not long enough, because it's not working fast enough. "

"I'm sure your doctor told you it takes at least three to four months for the medicines to kick in. In another month you should feel much better."

"He probably told me," I admitted, "but I think I stopped listening. How are *you* feeling today?" I switched the attention to Rene. I was tired of hearing my own story.

"I'm doing great. I've integrated yoga and meditation into a daily routine. Do you feel well enough to do anything physical? What do you do during the days?"

"Worry," I said.

"Worry's not good. What are you worried about?" Rene asked.

"Dying. My daughter. My life. The usual." I felt tears pooling in the corners of my eyes. Rude emotion swelled inside my chest, making it hard to breathe. My head hung down and I wanted to disappear from this intimate entanglement with a stranger. It felt like days since anyone had asked me how I felt. Peter had gotten comfortable with silence.

"Morgan, it'll get better. Really. Lupus is tricky. You just have to learn how to outsmart it."

Resisting the urge to regurgitate my list of things that ailed me including Valley Fever, I took a hint from Peter and said nothing. Rene and I breathed into the phone for too many seconds and then I said, "How do you outsmart something that takes over your whole body? Everything either hurts, is swollen or itches. I have these fucking sores all over my face…" I could hear myself whining. "You must know the drill."

"Well, I never had sores on my face. But I did have terrible arthritis pain for weeks. At one time, I couldn't even use my hands."

"Really?" I imagined how that could be worse than my sores. *What would I do with Rain if I couldn't use my hands? How would I drive myself to the doctor?* For a brief moment, I was grateful.

Rene continued, "My hands eventually got better with meds and therapy, but that shows you that everyone has a different version of Lupus. Have you ever read Louise Hay's book, 'You Can Heal Your Life'? Lupus is a very individualistic disease. It's *personal.*"

"And I'm taking it personally. No, I've haven't read it, but I actually remember my mother talking about it when I was a little girl."

"Did it help her?" Rene asked.

"I don't think so. She's dead."

Rene sounded embarrassed. "Oh, I'm so sorry."

"Not your fault. I'll check it out, anyway. I need to heal my life, badly."

Rene said, "I think you'll be surprised at some of the things that it says about our own part in manifesting disease. I'd like to send it to you as a little gift. Gifts always cheered me up when I was first diagnosed. Beauregard already gave me your address."

I was stunned at how the Healthy Girls took liberties – giving people's home addresses to complete strangers. "Oh. OK."

Rene continued. "Louise Hay's book suggests that when we're not honest with ourselves, our bodies get sick. Do you ever get to California?"

"Peter's aunt lives in Ladera Heights," I said picturing Gladys' suburban refuge.

"That's right outside of LA. I live in West Hollywood," Rene said.

"Why do you ask?"

"My holistic doctor, Dr. Lazard, is in Pacific Palisades. He has done wonders for me and I thought it would be great if you could get an appointment with him."

"I'm not that fond of doctors. What's so special about yours?"

"He's a holistic doctor, but *also* an MD. I think you'd like him."

Roy's voice shot into my mind. *Doctors will kill ya!* I finally said, "I probably can't afford him. Peter and I are struggling. Since the diagnosis, I've not been able to work. I used to manage a small recording studio here in Oro Valley, but they couldn't save my job for me when my doctors recommended six months off."

"That may be against the law. Did Beauregard tell you that I'm an attorney? An appointment with Dr. Lazard *is* expensive. It's $675 for the first appointment and $175 after that."

"Oh." I could hear Roy ranting, *675? 675! That's a month's rent. That's a mortgage payment! Doctors are crooks!* I said to Rene, "I don't know when I'll be in California next. But, if I get there, I'll let you know. What kind of an attorney are you?"

"Civil Rights and Discrimination. I work for the Cochran Firm.

It's against the law to fire someone for being sick. Would you like me to look into it for you?"

"No thank you, Rene. It wasn't the greatest job in the world. I just took it because it was music-related and music is all I know. It wasn't too hard to let go of when they said they couldn't keep my job. Did Beauregard tell you that I was in the music business?"

"She mentioned it, but she was much more concerned with your illness. She called me right away after you told her. I think Dr. Lazard could be good for you," said Rene.

"Doctors are all the same. They collect your co-pay before they even see your face, then they talk to you for about two minutes and prescribe a bunch of poisonous drugs and set up a follow-up appointment for four weeks. I hate them."

"I hear ya, girl. Dr. Lazard is different. He listens in a real way. He even takes notes while you talk. And then he lets you know, from hearing your story, why disease has manifested in your body. His appointments can go on for hours."

"I don't think I have ever heard of anything like that," I said, still unconvinced.

Well, there's lots more to tell, but I won't bore you, yet. All I can say is that I feel 100% better and I owe it all to Dr. Lazard, chile!" Rene said, enthusiastically.

After Rene assured me that she would be in touch and she would send the book, I lay back on the couch and thought about the oddness of her voice. She was soothing, nasal, and nagging all at the same time. I chuckled at Rene's spattering of black girl speak: "Girl", "I hear you" and "Chile" in the midst of her over-educated crispness. Her clash of two worlds was familiar and endearing. I wasn't sure that Rene and I would have anything in common except for our fancy educations and our failing bodies, but at that moment she was all I had.

I missed who I used to be and I was afraid of whom I was becoming. Music had started to irritate me. It took too much out of me to love it with my whole body, the way I once did. I needed to be rescued from the grip of this bitchy disease. I was curious about Rene's Dr. Lazard. I knew I needed to do something bigger than what my doctors were suggesting: take the pills and wait.

It was 3 a.m. and Peter had been out with Chad and the guys, when he stumbled into our bedroom and woke me up, reeking of too many cigars and too much 12-year old scotch.

"Morgan, I have to talk to you." The moon's light was blinding as it shone over the pool and blasted through the sheer curtains that hung over our bed.

I said, "What?"

He was sloppy as he said, "I realized something tonight. I want to be honest. Don't start cryin', Morgan. I don't want to be married, anymore. Don't take it personal." Then, he added, "It's not about you. It's about me."

The silence was as loud as a hundred-piece marching band. I sat up in bed and said what frightened women often say, "You don't mean that. You're drunk."

With a loud gasp, Peter's eyes swelled with tears. His shoulders began to shake as if currents were going through him. He couldn't look at me. He was a snake losing his skin. I took the hand that was not too stiff and slid my fingers through Peter's curls. I hadn't touched him this gently in years. Work, Greed, and Sickness had become our roadblocks. I gently slid my husband back onto his side of our king-sized bed and awkwardly removed his shoes and pants. My stiffened fingers struggled with the zipper as I tried hard not to disturb him. I wanted to offer Peter the safety of saying something he didn't mean without having to pay the hefty price of a wife's wrath. I lay back down on my side of our bed for the rest of the night, soothed by Peter's gentle snores which were like the purrings of a kitten. I prayed for the first time in a long time, wrestling with the two most dreadful thoughts: drunk people often say things that they don't mean. And, alcohol is called the truth serum.

The morning after, Peter and I both retreated into our respective corners; too ashamed of the ugliness that lay before us. After several quiet days had passed, Peter dared to go near the monstrous topic again. We were in the kitchen together, preparing Marigold's famous spaghetti sauce. I felt well enough to attempt making a dinner that Peter liked and would help me with. He was chopping onions and green peppers and I was removing the innards of the hot sausage from its casing.

Rain was sitting in her bright red high chair, fiddling with a multi-colored fuzz ball that she had chosen as her official plaything of the week. The only music was the sound of knives chopping and Rain cooing to herself. Peter knew that I couldn't stand the sound of the radio anymore. The startling noise that we both heard was Rain letting out a bloodcurdling wail. It seemed that she was trying to get another round of the Screaming Game started with me. With Peter there, there was no space for our only private pastime. I ignored Rain with a surreptitious smile. Peter dropped his knife, startled. When he saw Rain's toothless grin and neither blood nor cause for concern, Peter was not amused. He gave her a hard look and chastised sternly. "Stop that screamin', baby girl! You scared me." Rain obliviously smiled and extended her fuzz ball to Peter. Peter rudely ignored her offering and walked back to the onions and peppers. He said over his shoulder into the thick air, "I'm going through some kind of phase. I don't think I should be married. I just hate making you so unhappy. I'm unhappy, too. I think I forgot how to be happy."

I turned to face his back which was turned to me. "What the fuck are you saying?"

Rain looked startled. She was unfamiliar with that word and the muted siren of panic.

"I'm saying that I need space," he stumbled. "This phase will end. I'll want to be married again, as soon as I get through this phase of not wanting to be married."

My father's words immediately popped into my head and spouted out of my mouth, "That's bullshit. 'Don't let people piss in your face and tell you it's rain.'"

"Morgan, listen. Uncle Ezekiel went through this, too. He said a man has to stretch out sometime. Marriage gets routine. It's nothing against our wives. We love you but don't want to lose what made us men in the first place – the need to hunt. When Uncle Zeke told me that, it scared me. It still scares me. It made me think. I still need to be free. I'm sorry. Please be patient with me."

Just as he said that, Peter's eyes wandered for a split second and his finger got too close to the knife. The blade bit deeply into his finger, spilling redness all over the granite countertop and onto the tile floor.

I ignored his blood and shouted, "What the hell do you mean? You're a grown man with a daughter and a wife who both need you."

Peter moaned as blood oozed out of his thumb. I looked at him standing there with his thumb in his mouth. I despised him. I stormed out of the room with nowhere to go.

I remember when Peter wasn't cold. He was the warmest man I had ever met. I will never forget when he loved to snuggle and coo, like a baby desperate to express ineffable things. He once whispered in my ear, "I always dreamed that I would marry a beautiful, smart woman like you. You are so much more than my dream and because of that, I will call you "More."

Sadly, I had deteriorated into much less than either one of us could have imagined. I had become a stiff woman with crippled knees and a face splattered with pus-filled sores; leaning on walls when I was too weak to stand.

When Peter brushed past me in the bedroom in search of a band-aid, without looking back, he said, "Morgan, I just didn't sign up for this."

I could hear Rain in the kitchen alone, looking to see where we had gone.

Silence reigned except for the occasional fire starters. Every weekday Peter drove Rain to daycare in the mornings and picked her up, so I could rest and go to doctors' appointments. Peter rarely stayed home after he brought her home during the week. Peter was never home on weekends, either. During the week, I fed Rain, bathed her in the sink, and put her to bed. On the weekends, Rain and I played the Screaming Game which was the only thing I had energy for. I slept a lot while she drooled all over the tile floor trying to entertain herself. Our lives carried the tension of a waiting room; neither of us knowing who would be called away first.

Another week after the spaghetti dinner discussion, Peter walked into the house and asked, "Is there a cure for your mouth?" His face was twisted into a sneer.

I met him at the door and took a squirming Rain out of his arms. "What are you talking about?"

"Chad asked me on the golf course today what was happening to us. You must've mentioned something to his wife, Laura. Be honest,

Morgan. Did you say that we were having problems? Did you tell her that you're sick?" Peter looked pained.

I said, "I did, because I am."

I *had* said something to Laura. And Cheryl, and Amy and Dawn.

Chad's wife and I had struggled to find a common thread between us. Our husbands wanted us to be friends so that they could be. Laura didn't work. I had been a workaholic all of my life. Peter and I only had one child while Laura and Chad had three boys and a nanny. Peter had desperately wanted me to befriend Laura to close the chasm of our lives. I so desperately wanted Peter's love the way I remembered it. I was willing to do anything.

The bruising words had tumbled out at the luncheon that the Oro Valley wives called S&L, Salads and Lemonade. In my mind, I renamed them "Snobs and Lushes." Their lemonade was always spiked with vodka. The wives of S&L met the third Thursday of every month at one of the desert houses in the Tortolita Mountains, where we all lived. Peter and I had been to Chad and Laura's five-bedroom, three-story stucco house on several occasions. Their view of the Valley always reinforced why we chose Oro Valley as our home. On the day that the ladies of S&L were meeting, my face was clearer than it had been in months. I decided to go, knowing that Peter would be glad to see me off the couch and with the friends that he wanted me to have.

I timidly entered the familiar cathedral-ceilinged great room, dreading the shocked expressions that I anticipated. At first, they said nothing, until Laura gave them permission, with her own scrutiny.

"Morgan, you look different. You've lost a lot of weight, haven't you?"

"You look fabulous," said another one of the wives, without looking up.

Another of the foothills wives noticed that I had stopped caring for my once short natural hair that was always barbered into a smart stylish cut. "I just love what you're doing to your hair. It's so funky and wild." *Marigold would have called it unkempt.*

"Hello, ladies," I finally responded to all of the unwanted attention that was coming at me like darts. "Sorry, I've been out of the loop. I've been having some trouble with my knees."

I walked with my new slow gait, praying not to stumble from weakness. I sat on the leather couch closest to where I was standing. I sat alone, worrying that I may still smell of the odious tea tree oil that I rubbed on my joints at the advice of a holistic Lupian.

I listened to the wives' conversation, trying hard to care about the things that they did: private schools, nannies, housekeepers, birthday parties, ski resorts, and pool guys. I wanted to jump in and say something that would make me one of them. I no longer possessed the ability to scintillate in the company of the rich. *The Eastside days were gone.* My otherness was conspicuous. I sipped water instead of lemonade to appease my dry throat. The girls of S&L smirked at my prudishness. I was nauseated by the limp salad drowning in mud-brown balsamic vinaigrette. I cringed at the thought of acid in my raw sore-filled mouth. I politely rested the crystal salad plate on the glass table in front of me, gripping the cold water, hoping it would calm my perpetual low-grade fever.

The conversation took a turn. The wives complained about their husbands as they picked at their salads and gulped down their lemonades.

"Paul never eats dinner with us, anymore."

"George is always traveling."

"John is training for a marathon; he's tired all the time. You know what that means for our sex life…"

"Chad's never home anymore," Laura said through her pink glossed lips. "It's like he's MIA. That's because he's always out smokin' flippin' cigars with Peter Holmes!" Laura tossed her thin red hair out of her eyes and smiled at me with an impish grin.

I heard myself chime in. "I know, Laura. Maybe when Peter moves out, he and Chad could room together. Peter's no use to us anyway."

I did talk. I talked too much. Peter detested that about me.

The phones rang constantly and my desktop overflowed with emails. The Lupians were always checking in and filing their latest complaints. Karla emailed me once a week to offer new holistic cures. Deborah texted me with foods to avoid. Rene was the most persistent, checking in several times a week. I was surprised to see her name again on my caller ID. She had just called a couple of days before.

"Hello?" I said cautiously, hoping she wasn't calling about that Doctor Lazard, whom I couldn't afford.

"Morgan, it's Rene. How ya doin'? I'm just checking in on you because you sounded so upset the other day."

"I feel a little better today. Like you said, every day I feel a miniscule improvement. My face cleared up a little and I even ventured out to lunch."

"Did you enjoy it? What did you eat?"

"I probably shouldn't have gone. I looked awful and my knee is still stiff. I didn't eat anything. I wasn't hungry. I had sores in my mouth again. But at least I was not on the couch or in bed."

"That's my girl! Morgan, it'll get better. Don't push yourself too much, but just keep tryin' a little every day."

"Thanks for the reminder. What's up?"

"I just wanted to check in and tell you that I popped the book in the mail last night. You'll get it in a couple of days. I really can't wait to hear what you think."

"I'll let you know. Didn't you say that you're working again part-time?"

"Yeah. I'm working a lot from home since this case is a high-profile hate crime case and it's pro bono. The firm takes a lot of cases from the black community. We're trying to build trust. You know black folks don't trust lawyers."

"What's the case about?" I asked, grateful to be talking about something other than my health.

"Typical. Young black gay man was beaten and shot to death by a group of straight guys. I wanted to get the NAACP involved but the firm worried that the churches would retaliate because we would be defending homosexuality by taking the hate crime angle. We are not defending anything but a human's right to live. It's a hard case to do, but I feel for the family. Now that I have thoroughly depressed us both, how are things with you?"

"That sounds terrible. Church people should be ashamed of themselves. Speaking of shame, the latest is that Peter says he's going through a phase."

"What kind of phase? Do tell."

"A not-wanting-to-be-married-anymore phase," I said slowly trying to let it sink in.

"Now? When you're sick?" Rene sounded as though her mouth was open.

"He lacks timing," I said.

"He's got to care about timing. It could make you sicker, Morgan. I'm so sorry that you're dealing with Lupus and a trippin' husband."

"I can't really care about the trippin' husband anymore. I just want to feel better. I'm envious that you can even work. I couldn't work even if they saved my job. I'm so tired, it feels like I have mud running through my body."

"Remember, I can look into this thing at your job. What's the name of the place again?" Rene asked.

"Moonsong Studios," I said. "But really, Rene, don't bother. Everything's about to change. That's the only thing I'm certain of."

CHAPTER 6 | *Leaving*

When Peter came home that evening, I felt better. Talking to Rene about her work at the firm reminded me that there were other pressing things in the world. Speaking to someone other than myself reminded me of how self-pitying I had become. I was grateful for all of the calls, texts, and emails. I felt loved from a distance, but I still craved real human contact: laughter, affection and conversation. I had been stranded.

Rene and Dr. Lazard were everywhere my brain traveled. My body had finally started to quiet. Random places weren't swelling as often and my knees and hands were looser. I felt better, but the tease of slight wellness made me ravenous for feeling authentically good. I didn't want my healing to be credited solely to the poisons of doctors. Roy always said 'doctors will kill you.' Roy was always right.

When Peter entered the house with Rain on his shoulder, he stepped lightly, trying to bring Rain in without waking her. Melancholy swept over me. When Peter mouthed the words "take her" with a deadpan face, it used to be the start of a humorous routine that we had created. Since the diagnosis, he looked at me only with a pitiful smile that he had designed just for the sick me. I took Rain silently to her room.

My pregnancy and the birth of Rain had brought new energy to the marriage. Peter was an adoring husband. Rubbing my feet at night, giving me scalp massages, and bringing me seaweed which I craved throughout the pregnancy. After she was born, Peter and I started to mime instead of speak to each other so that we wouldn't wake her. The clownish faces that Peter created would always hurl me into muffled hysterical laughter. Just the memory of his bulging eyes and flailing tongue saddened me because our silly bliss reminded me how far apart we had grown. Miraculously, Rain never stirred in those days. The sound of *happyfamily* must have lulled her.

We'd made an agreement that whoever was responsible for waking her would serve a full breakfast in bed the next morning to the other and perform all of Rain's morning chores: feeding, bathing, packing the diaper bag, and choosing her outfit for the first half of the day. Peter and I used to say to each other, "A lot is at stake." We feigned dread although there was nothing either of us would rather do than serve each other and our daughter. *It was a whole other lifetime.*

I put Rain into her crib and walked back into the living room. Peter had poured himself a scotch and water and he signaled the empty glass on the counter with a shaky finger offering me a drink. I picked up the glass, wishing for something stronger, but filled my glass with filtered water from the refrigerator door.

"Maybe it's timing." Peter approached the Monster again, the beast intent on destroying our marriage. "Maybe we *are* in the wrong place at the wrong time. Oro Valley sucks. I'm hangin' on by a thread. I don't know what to do, Morgan. Maybe we both need time to figure it all out." Peter's face was blank.

"What are you suggesting?" I asked, bracing myself for the clamor of the marching band.

"I would leave, but I have to work. It's easier for you to go away. Would you consider going away for a short while? I just really need some space. I think we both do."

"You're asking me to leave? Why would I do that? I'm sick, Peter, did you forget? Where the hell would I go?" I snapped.

"How 'bout going to visit Aunt Gladys? She wants to help take care of you, anyway. She's lonely without Uncle Zeke. Don't worry about the cost of the ticket."

I could use a change of scenery, I thought. I was rotting in the house with no human contact except for Rain, who was as dangerous to my well-being as she was critical. Every cough she brought home from daycare was a potential setback for me.

"So what do you think?" Peter dragged me out of my thoughts.

I finally said, "How far is Ladera Heights from West Hollywood?"

"Who do you know in West Hollywood?" Peter demanded, as if I had a lover there.

"I have a friend," I said proudly.

"Who?"

"Rene Harden."

"Who the hell is Rene Harden?"

"She's got Lupus, too," I said.

"It's not far. It's about a 20-30 minute drive without traffic. I'm sure Aunty would take you to visit her, if you wanted."

"Rene has a holistic doctor that she wants me to meet. She'll try to get me an appointment if she knows I'll be in California. We've been talking about it. "

Peter's tone switched to annoyance. "All you do is talk. How much will that cost? Holistic doctors are a fortune. Morgan, you're killin' me with all of your expensive ideas. Why can't you stick to the doctors that my insurance pays for? I can't afford all this shit."

"Peter, you're the one who's asking me to leave my own house. It's none of your business what I do and who I see while I'm there. As far as the holistic doctor goes, I have to try everything. Some of the holistic stuff I've tried has actually worked. I don't care how much it costs. Conventional doctors will keep giving me more and more poison and I will eventually get sicker than when I started."

"You can't go away for too long, you know," he said as he walked to the other side of the island. "Rain needs you. You're her mom. Or did you forget that?"

"I never forget that. That's why I'm so desperate to get well." I could feel myself shaking. "I want to be a good mother who can care for her like a mother should. I need to go for two to three weeks. It depends on if and when Rene can get the appointment with Dr. Lazard for me."

"That's too long," Peter said adamantly.

"Why? It's just enough time for you to think and I can see this doctor and find out if he can help me. Besides what do you care? I thought you were going through a phase. Give me a break, Peter. Free me. I need time as much as you do."

"What about Rain?" Peter was shaking his head and looking down at the tile floor.

"I'll take her," I said.

"I'm going through a phase, but a wife never leaves her husband for a long period. Three weeks is too long."

"Too bad. Book it. I'll call Rene and see about her getting the appointment."

I walked out of the room to reflect on what I had just done. The thought of lying on the couch for another minute with an invisible spouse made me feel desperate. Somewhere inside I was angry. I wanted to stay, but I couldn't. I wanted to go but I was scared. Thoughts of traveling alone with Rain gave me a headache, remembering the trip to New York. But Rain was my anchor and both she and I needed to get away from all that was broken.

Peter's Aunt Gladys was a self-proclaimed expert on marriage. She had coached me on my wedding day. "The key to a marriage that lasts forever is to understand that your husband always knows best."

Her eyes had filled with tears thinking about Ezekiel's death. At least in Gladys' eyes by going away for a while, I would be doing what Peter thought was best. I could no longer see straight. My own vision had become blurred.

I looked at the calendar hanging on the side of the refrigerator, held up with magnets shaped like business cards from plumbers and electricians. The calendar was filled with red and green lines and circles. The red indicated the doctor's appointments: the green when it was time to get blood taken. I had been going to the doctor almost weekly for months, the appointments were finally slowing.

I looked at a date three weeks out and called Rene to tell her that was when I would be coming.

Before Rene could answer the phone, when I heard her pick up, I jumped in anxiously, "Rene, Peter says that Ladera Heights is not too far from West Hollywood."

"Who's this?" Rene sounded confused.

"It's me, Morgan. I'm coming to California."

Rene's voice warmed. "How did you make that happen so fast?"

"Well, let's just say Peter's being generous and he suggested that we both need some time away. I'll be bringing my daughter, so we'll stay with Peter's Aunt Gladys. She can help me take care of Rain," I said, feeling more confident about the plan with every word that I spoke.

"When are you comin'?" Rene asked.

"I was hoping that you could get me an appointment with Dr. Lazard. I think I can be there in about three weeks. First, I have to go see all of my doctors to check in, but I think they'll let me."

"That's marvelous news, Morgan. You can always stay with me, if Aunt Gladys gets to be too much."

"Thanks for the offer…Maybe when I go to Dr. Lazard I can stay with you for a night or two. Then we can hang out and have fun." Fun seemed like something I hadn't had or even said in so long that the word felt clumsy coming out.

"That sounds good, Morgan. I'll get on the phone now and try to get an appointment. We'll patch up the details when it gets closer. I'm excited for you to meet him. I know he'll help you."

"I'm excited to meet *you*," I said, thrilled that an ally was waiting.

I heard Peter approaching the house. He had his hands full with Rain, and I needed to get off the phone. Peter always sneered at me when I was on the phone when he walked in.

"Who was that?" Peter wanted to know as Rain smiled and reached for me. "Raindrop, we're goin' on a trip, we're goin' on a trip!" I sang to her in a child-like melody.

"It was Rene."

I kissed Rain and took her from Peter's arms. "Did you call Gladys yet to tell her that we're coming?"

"I told her. She's thrilled," Peter said.

"All I have to do now is get the OK from Dr. Valdez, Dr. Tron, and Dr. White – to see if they're OK with it."

"I still think three weeks is too long," Peter said as he took a seat on the couch.

"Why do you care? You haven't cared since I got back from New York," I yelled.

"I do care and I'm tired of hearing you accuse me of not caring. I go to work every single day and provide you with health insurance. That's caring."

I walked back into the room and whispered, "Somehow it's just not enough. I need your face in my face. I need to feel that you still love me although my face changes every day. I need you to stay home just because I live here and I need you."

Tears were streaming down my face. I felt the weight in my chest start to lighten.

Startled by my sudden tears, Peter said, "More, I'll work on it. I want to be better for you. Please just give me this space. While you're gone, I'll get my act together. I'll be the husband and father you want me to be when you come back. I won't disappoint you."

Peter booked the flight that night. I was scheduled to leave for Los Angeles in 15 days. The fear and anticipation made me feel alive again. I was going to *fly*.

Lupians are not supposed to fly because of our pill-induced compromised immune systems. When I told Dr. Valdez of my plans, he frowned but reluctantly agreed to it. He sensed my desperation to make a single decision for myself after months of being controlled by him and his colleagues.

I refilled all of my prescriptions. I also got the name and phone number of the pharmacy closest to Gladys's house. The pharmacist agreed that he would honor my Oro Valley prescriptions. I even assured Dr. Valdez that I would wear a mask on the plane. I had been housebound for six months; by boarding that plane for Los Angeles I would no longer be a lady-in-waiting.

The week before the trip I was on the edge of my nerves. I cried because I felt like I was being evicted. I cried when I thought of the flight and feared Rain squirming in my arms and my not having enough strength to contain her. I shuddered at the thought of forgetting my expensive holistic potions: Arnica, tea tree oil and my Castor Oil Packs. I cried because I would miss my huge bed that had become my only comfort. I cried because I knew deep down that this was the beginning of the end of *this* life.

The day of the flight, I prayed no one on the plane would have a cough or some other condition I could catch. I had purchased a box of deluxe surgical masks, but was ashamed of how I would appear to other people with the sky blue paper mask on my face. *"What's wrong with her?"* I imagined people would whisper.

Gladys had told me how to arrange for wheelchair service. On the morning of the flight, Peter took Rain and me to the airport. At the gate, he shoved $50 dollars into my hand with a meaningless kiss to my forehead, while he showered Rain with kisses, hugs, and squeezes. I was jealous of her.

"Rain, be a sweet girl for Mommy and Gladdy. Tell Gladdy I said hello!" Rain listened, laughed and flashed her famous grin. Since Aunt Gladys was not really Peter's mother, he came up with a name for Gladys that would make her feel like she had a grandchild, even thought it was really a grandniece. Gladys loved the name. She bragged to the ladies at church, I am a Gladmother!

I felt like kicking the air and screaming that I didn't want to go, but I accepted Peter's insult to my forehead and wallet and waited patiently to be wheeled onto the plane with my daughter on my lap and all the other senior citizens and disabled people following behind us in slow motion. We boarded the plane like limos in a funeral procession.

Rain and I found our seat in the first row of coach. I waited patiently for everyone else to sit before considering the dreaded task of donning the mask. Smelling the jet fuel always excited me on a cellular level, reminding me that I was going places. Rain frowned at the strong smell and scrunched up her nose. I put my knapsack on the seat next to me, hoping that no one would sit there and I wouldn't need the mask at all. The empty seat beside me was my backup plan in case I had to put her down. Although she was still young enough to be considered a lap child, Rain was so squirmy that holding her was as impossible as trying to hold on to Peter, whose only desire was to be free. Just as the plane's doors were closing and it appeared that Rain and I were home free, a woman approached us. "Is there anyone sitting in that seat?" I had no choice but to say no. I begrudgingly took my bag off the seat.

The slender woman looked healthy. She was casually dressed in jeans, a T-shirt, and a sweater draped around her shoulders. She had shoulder-length graying hair that suited her youthful and pretty face. She had ethnic turquoise and silver jewelry on, dangling from her ears and wrists. She didn't wear a watch. She smiled politely at Rain as she crossed in front of me and sat down at the window seat.

Across the aisle and one seat behind me was another mother with a little boy about Rain's age. The woman was engrossed in her book. It was "You Can Heal Your Life," the book that Rene had sent me. I had it in my bag, planning to get to it while I was at Gladys'. I hoped the book was engrossing enough that this woman wouldn't want to talk. I loved her in advance for her silence.

She read about three pages of the book with complete absorption. We were still on the runway and Rain had noticed the boy behind us and was desperate to peer over my shoulder to get a better look at him. I sat consumed and gloomy with fear, anger and confusion, while Rain hung over my shoulder to see her new friend.

And then the woman coughed.

The first one was simply her clearing her throat.

I patted my bag knowing the mask was inside.

She read two more pages in silence.

And then, an all-out hacking cough burst from her mouth.

I panicked.

Was she a smoker? She seemed too health-conscious to smoke. Was this the cough of someone with the flu? The common cold? A communicable disease? Did she have TB? *She was reading "You Can Heal Your Life" for Godssakes!*

Then came the phlegm and a handful of tissues emerged from her lengthy, piano-player fingers. She had concealed the tissues when she sat down; the book was the only clue that she may not be as healthy as she appeared.

I reluctantly pulled out my surgical mask as the flight attendant started to recite the safety instructions. I was hoping all eyes would be glued to the pretty flight attendant who was stumbling all over her words. Just as I had the baby blue surgical mask adjusted to my nose, the boy in the row behind us started to cough. I knew Rain would follow suit. Unfortunately, I had taught her to mimic. The boy and Rain both barked an unidentifiable daycare cough at each other. The boy's cough was real, I feared. Rain was just playing, I prayed.

I secured my mask and tried to calm myself by rocking Rain on my one good knee. I donned my mirrored sunglasses, baseball cap and held Rain with one arm. I withdrew into a cloud of silence. I thought about Peter and the thing that he had promised, "in sickness and in health." I remembered how Peter said that his Aunt and Uncle didn't believe in divorce because they were Christians. I thought of Roy and Marigold and how they had done the right thing by divorcing. They didn't drag each other through the indignities of marital humiliation. I stared at the clouds fearing the cough and praying to wake up in a different state of mind.

The wheelchair attendant came right to my seat, took Rain from me, held my backpack on her shoulder and with her free arm, offered to get me into the wheelchair. The Valley Fever knee was still bothering me. I was limping only slightly but the long walk through LAX was the reason for the chair. I walked about three feet to the wheelchair, which was right at the door of the plane. As the attendant rolled Rain and I off the jetway, I saw Gladys waiting at the gate, just as she'd promised.

My gloom deepened at the sight of her. Gladys was weighted down with all the accoutrements of a church lady. She wore a huge hat, a big smile, heavy make-up, and floral perfume that made my nose scrunch up the way Rain's had when she smelled the jet fuel. She was a vision of paleness. Her face showed how deeply unsatisfied she was. Aunt Gladys was an empty well without her husband. Gladys was nothing like Marigold and I often felt Marigold would not have approved of Aunt Gladys as a mother figure for me, but she was all I had.

Gladys stood as decorated as a fictional queen with her fake corsage on her lapel and her reddish wig tightly glued to her head. Gladys's color-coded corsages indicated the days of the week. Today's was deep purple.

Like a blanket covering my mouth and nose, Gladys' floral scent smothered me. "Morgan! Rain! Hello! I'm so glad to see you both." As she spoke, she gently nudged the attendant out of the way and said, "Thank you, Miss. Have a good day." She handed her a wrinkled one dollar bill and said, "Get yourself a soda."

It all happened so fast that I realized I was already several feet from the attendant who stood there staring at the bill with disgust. I looked back regretfully and whispered as sincerely as possible, "Thank you so much!" The attendant's back was where my words landed.

"Morgan, you don't look *so* bad. By the grace of God, you must be feeling so much better."

"I do feel a little better."

Gladys talked incessantly as she rolled us to baggage claim. She sprayed us with words, sucking very little air in between each one. The chaos of the airport swirled around me as I sat in the mist of her scent. I could faintly hear her, "Rainy-Rain! Gla-a-ad-d-d-y is so happy to see you. You've grown so much! What happened to my Rainy-Rain? Look at how long your hair has grown," she said to her while hovering over my shoulders reaching towards my lap to touch her.

She finally switched her attention to me. "Morgan, I'm going to cook you all of your favorite foods. You just need to gain some weight. Peter said that you were wasting away."

"Peter's not the greatest cook," I said smiling.

"That's alright. I'm here now and happy to have you both." As Gladys talked at us, I stayed quiet and allowed my mind to wander to how tired I felt, not physically, but mentally. I was eager to be back at the house where Peter grew up. Gladys' house was always pristine, reeking of bleach and air freshener. Her refrigerator was always full of plastic containers filled with leftovers because she still made dinners for two even though Ezekiel had been dead for years.

I shuddered at how I paled in comparison to her as a wife. I had always consoled myself with the fact that I made money. Gladys' long career as a nurse should have reduced her wifely duties that were laid out in the Christian Wife guidebook that she followed to the letter. *I could never get through the first page.* As if she had been able to see into the future, Aunt Gladys was a straight shooter. The first time I went to visit Peter in Ladera Heights, she had looked straight into my eyes over dinner and said, "Morgan, I'm totally underwhelmed by you."

CHAPTER 7 | *Quicksand*

Los Angeles, California November 2004

We rolled out of LAX in Aunt Gladys' new purple sedan. Rain had behaved as though she understood that I couldn't handle too much stress. I was relieved and proud of her.

As we hit the freeway, Gladys turned down the gospel station and said to me with a preacher's rigor, "Morgan, you know I'll always be a mother figure to you. Just like I am to Peter. No matter what happens to you and my Peacock, I will always be in your life. Don't ever forget that."

Gladys and I had worked diligently to create a relationship that we all could live with, despite her being underwhelmed by me from day one. Peter had once screamed at her, "You're not even my mother, who are you to judge me?" Gladys immediately sought counseling from Pastor Jackson who told her to let Peter live his own life and make his own choices. Since then, Gladys had changed. Not wanting to lose the only "son" she would ever have, she had grown into cooing and fussing over me as if I were her own daughter. That fated summer that Peter's biological mom got into trouble, Gladys was secretly relieved. God made her a mother just like she had asked him to.

"Thanks, Glad" I said, the last word falling clumsily out of my mouth. Peter had begged me to call her that. At least he didn't ask me to call her Mom. I couldn't have brought myself to do it with the taunting images of Marigold dancing in my head. When Gladys referred to me as her daughter, I could feel Marigold reluctantly but willfully giving me permission to embrace the mother figure that life handed me as a default. *You can't choose your family.*

Ladera Heights is an oasis of the African American upper middle class. From my metallic silver seat, everything about Peter's upbringing made sense.

"Is this a new car?" I asked, desperate for smaller talk.

"It is! It's a limited edition sedan that was created especially for my sorority. They only made 500 of them and only in California. I hate to brag but my chapter is pretty powerful around here. When a large group of black professional married women come together, we have a lot of power. When we approached the car dealer, they agreed to send a proposal to corporate and when it was approved they actually created this limited edition sedan for our sorority. You know that purple and silver are our colors. I just had to have one of these cars. Don't you love it?" Gladys asked, admiring the glaring metallic seats. I had been alarmed by the ghastly purple exterior as soon as I saw it, but it was so Gladys. Being with Gladys in her purple-and-silver world was like landing on the moon. It was difficult to breathe.

It was time for me to compliment her. So, I did. "It's gorgeous, Glad. I love it!"

Gladys stared straight ahead at the lunchtime traffic. She ignored my compliment and grew serious again. "You know, Morgan, illness in a marriage often destroys it."

"Do you think that's what's going to destroy our marriage?" I asked, bracing myself for her unruly candor.

"No, dear. Not at all. My Peacock loves you and Rain to pieces," she said.

So why am I here with you and not in my own house with my husband caring for me? I wondered, but all I said was "I know he does." Peacock is a nickname that she gave Peter when he was six years old. She had refused to retire it, even in mixed company. Peter refused to ask her to stop. He sort of reveled in it.

"He does love you, but you know that Peacock has a hard time handling things that are difficult. This time apart from you and Rain will make him see how important his family is and I know he'll be stronger than ever when you get back. In the meantime, I'm here to help you all. The Lord has blessed me with the strength to do it. And He's going to bless you, too."

"Did I just see a sign for West Hollywood?" I asked, gazing greedily at my temporary new surroundings.

"Yes, you would exit over there." Her arm crossed my face as she pointed out toward the East, I had to duck my head down to get out of the way of her floppy arm. "Why do you ask?"

"Didn't Peter tell you that I have a friend that may get me an appointment with her holistic doctor?"

"A holistic doctor? You know I don't really believe in those kinds of things." She quickly self-corrected. "It's not wrong. It's just not right for me."

"My friend, Rene, also has Lupus and she says that this doctor helped her a lot," I said.

"Well, the Lord is going to get rid of your Lupus because He knows you have Miss Rainy-Rain to raise and my Peacock to take care of. With the right food and a calm, relaxing environment, you'll be good as new. But I will gladly take you to visit your friend. Just let me know when you want to go and I'll get you there. What kind of girl is she? Is she married?" Gladys asked.

"No, she's not married. Maybe she was. I never asked. She's an attorney."

"Well, that's impressive. Perfect place for her to find a nice lawyer husband," Gladys said.

"When I get to the house, I'd like to let her know I'm here."

"What do you want for lunch?" Gladys asked.

"You decide. I'm just happy to be here. Being with you makes me feel better, Glad. "

"Well that's what I'm here for."

When we arrived at the sky blue stucco house, Gladys ran around to my side of the car and opened the door for me. She extended her arm for me to use while I dismounted from the spaceship-like seat. "We're here," she said.

"Happy to be here," I responded.

"You just go on in and I will bring in the bags and the baby. Do you still have your key?" Gladys asked.

I fished around in the bottom of my bag for the key Aunt Gladys had presented to me on my wedding day in a glass box with the security code to the house taped to the bottom. Peter had told me in advance that the easy way to remember the code is that it spelled J-e-s-u-s on the keypad.

I finally found the key, slipped it into the lock and punched in the code. I stepped in to the familiar wave of floral scented air freshener and the unforgettable sight of leather Bibles stacked at the door. There was a new one on top, a small Bible covered in baby blue leather with the name *Rain Holmes* in gold lettering in the lower corner.

I walked into the room where Rain and I would be staying. Gladys came in through the garage with Rain in her arms. She handed her to me and said, "I'll bring the bags in and get started on lunch."

I sat on Peter's lumpy high school bed. He had chosen the lower-level room for its proximity to the TV room, the front door, and the garage. Peter had bragged many times about how that room facilitated late night escapes to go drink with his friends and steal unsuspecting girls in and out of the house.

The room held on stubbornly to the smell of musty male: athletic socks, cotton t-shirts, and years of unwashed jeans to preserve the color. The pungent scent of Gladys's Clorox had battled with teenage boy scent and lost. Gladys had set up a crib in the corner of the room with sheets adorned with fairies and stars and a mobile over the crib with brightly colored scented fuzz balls. Rain crawled on the shag carpet looking in all the corners, as if she too, was seeking clues to the Holmes family mystery.

I closed my eyes briefly when I heard Gladys singing "Mor-gan, lunch is ready for you and Rainy. Come on!"

I approached the white laminate tablecloth and saw that Gladys had made my favorites: tuna sandwiches on multigrain toast with sweet potato fries.

"I know that you're not supposed to eat dairy products, so I skipped the cheese and I know how much you love French fries, so I made sweet potato fries. Instead of salt, I used cinnamon."

It was like a gift. The warmth of the meal filled me up inside and I was strangely thankful to Peter for getting me off the couch and out of my rut.

For Rain, Gladys had prepared crackers with jam and jelly and some grapes that she had cut up in tiny pieces that she planned to feed to her.

I ate with vigor, tasting Gladys's love and care which was in every bite. Gladys was born to be a mother only her body didn't know it. She was able to love anyone, even the "underwhelming."

"Morgan, I need to apologize to you."

"For what?" I asked my mouth full of sandwich anticipating the apology that I had waited years to hear.

"For Peter's behavior. I know he has not taken the best care of you during this difficult time."

You're damned right! Why is he treating me this way? I wanted to say, but I listened instead, realizing that she would never apologize for being "underwhelmed."

"You can never tell my Peacock that I spoke these words to you. Do you promise?"

"I promise," I said.

My late husband, Ezekiel, I'm afraid, was not a good role model for Peter," Gladys said sadly.

"What do you mean? Peter loved his uncle."

"It's really my fault. I shouldn't blame any of this on Zeke. Poor Zeke is not here to defend himself. When Peter's mother got stuck in Jamaica and I had to raise Peter, I was ecstatic. When Zeke's brother fell on hard times, his two boys came to live with us temporarily, too. I shouldn't have agreed to it. Raising three boys was not easy. And Zeke was not around much after they came. He was happiest when we were a family of three. When the boys came, he started staying away from home. At night he would complain to me that three boys was too much. Peter was always his favorite. It was the two nephews that took Zeke away from us. I let him do pretty much whatever he wanted to just to keep the peace in the family. His absence and distance harmed all of us. I never said a word."

"Why would a woman as smart as you do that?"

"I don't know, really. I guess it was how I was raised. I just never made him take accountability for the things that he did that hurt us and because I wanted to please Zeke, I wanted his brother to think well of me. To see that I was willing to help out a family member.

Since we didn't have children of our own, the family always looked at us as the ones to help. They took advantage of us. The boys' mother never took them back. She moved to Florida. Changed her name and her number. We couldn't find her anywhere. We eventually stopped looking. I didn't want to say too much about the boys but I knew they are what drove Zeke away from us. Now that he's gone, all I have left is Peter. The boys have drifted away too. They found women and are having kids of their own now."

"What was your husband doing all those years?"

"It's hard to explain, Morgan. I shouldn't say anymore."

Rain bellowed with a perfect Screaming Game pitch and slammed her sippy cup on the table, as though she, too, wanted Gladys to continue.

"Morgan, my mother always taught me that when a woman is lucky enough to get her a husband she should do everything in her power to keep him. So I ignored a lot of Ezekiel's faults. I just wanted to tell you these things because I think Peacock modeled after his uncle. He never learned the skills to cope with difficult things."

"Glad, my problems with Peter have nothing to do with you or your late husband."

"Morgan, I'm afraid your problems at home have everything to do with Peacock imitating what he grew up seeing. Ezekiel just didn't know how to take care of us, emotionally. When things went wrong, Ezekiel would just disappear." She paused for a moment while she put some more pieces of grape into Rain's open mouth. "He would go out to the bar with his friends or to the Mason's lodge. Or he would be out with his so-called women friends until things blew over at home. I would always pretend it wasn't happening and most importantly I acted as though it didn't bother me. I would just clean more, cook more and hope that eventually he would come back home."

This was no surprise to me. I had watched and listened carefully to Gladys over the course of my visits to California, looking for the root of Peter's sickly sweet goodness and her relentless adoration of Zeke. I just didn't know that Gladys actually understood what she was doing. She was such a good actress.

Gladys poured more lemon water into my drained glass. "Times have changed," she went on. "When Zeke and I were first married, Black folks didn't seek counseling or therapy of any kind when they had problems or one person was unhappy. Especially the wife. We were too ashamed to admit anything was wrong with us – we had been hearing something was wrong with us from too many other people. We all just went to church and prayed for a better outcome. You never questioned your husband. You just cleaned up his messes... with bleach," she added with a lame smile.

Rain had finished eating and was looking at me to get her out of her high chair. I stood and was able to lift her effortlessly.

Gladys was still speaking, her plate barely touched. "My own mother was deeply depressed, popping pills all the time to keep a smile on her face. She ran her own husband off with too much back talk and too many opinions. She begged me never to make the same mistake or else I'd be left alone just like she was. My mother always said a family without a head is not a whole."

"Do you think that's true?" I asked her as Rain bobbed up and down on my lap. "Glad, you lost your husband to untimely death. Do you feel like your life is no longer whole without him?"

"Only sometimes." Gladys averted her eyes.

I had six sweet potato fries left on my plate. I had saved them for last because they were so good, but my appetite had slipped away. Suddenly, I didn't want Gladys as a mother figure. I yearned for Marigold's strength to leave a man who was no good for her. I pitied Gladys. Tears started to roll from her eyes, plunging deeply into her purple corsage.

"What do you think I should do now?" I asked after a long silence.

"Morgan, because I never knew what to do in my own marriage, I give you permission to make your own decision. I'll love you whatever you do."

"I should help you clean up this kitchen," was the first thing that came to my racing mind.

Gladys dried her eyes with her apron and said, "I'll do the dishes. You take Rain in for her nap."

She stood before me with her arms outstretched. With Rain on my hip, I walked into her open arms and sank deeply into her full bosom; the corsage had sagged.

Gladys cleared the table and cleaned up the kitchen, then cleaned herself up to go get groceries for dinner. It was Thursday which meant fried chicken, broccoli, mashed potatoes, and gravy. That had been the set menu for 20 years of Thursdays. Although Zeke had been dead for several years, she still kept the same routine.

When Gladys appeared in the doorway to announce that she was ready, her red wig was back in place, her corsage stood at attention and her face bore that winning Holmes plastic smile. She peered in the door and said, "Can I take Rain with me? In case I run into someone I know, I can show off my gorgeous gladbaby."

"Sure. She couldn't sleep with all the excitement of the trip. Here's her diaper bag and a light jacket. She shouldn't get hungry but here are some more crackers just in case," I said. I turned to her and said, "Bye-bye, baby girl. Be a good girl for your Gladdy."

"Thank you, Morgan for listening. Goodbye, love. We'll see you soon." Suddenly a dreamy look came over her wrinkled face. The tone of her voice seemed slightly higher, "Zeke always got home at 6 on the dot and dinner would be almost finished by then." She smiled. "He liked to see his dinner still cooking when he got home, so he didn't worry that it had been on the stove too long. Zeke and all of those rules of his..." she said shaking her head.

Once again, the thoughts re-surfaced, the ones I'd stifled when I first met Peter in the airport. *He's too different from me.* It kept rushing through my head and I kept ignoring it. I washed those thoughts away with happier notions of family and suburban bliss. I suddenly had a bad taste in my mouth that I needed to spit out.

As soon as they were gone, I called Peter's cell phone to let him know we'd arrived. He didn't answer. I left a terse message, one I hoped wouldn't reflect my anxiety over when or if he'd get around to calling me back.

My phone rang immediately after leaving the message. I hoped it was Peter being responsive like he was when we first met. Instead, it was Rene. "I was just about to call you," I answered when I saw her name on caller ID.

"Great news! I was able to get you in with Dr. Lazard. He can squeeze you in next week, on Tuesday afternoon."

That's too soon, I thought. "Thanks Rene. I still need to call my father and ask him to send me the money. Hopefully I'll have it by then. My father doesn't believe in express anything. He sends everything by snail mail. He says the world goes too fast."

"No worries. I can lend it to you," Rene said.

"Thank you. That's really generous. I'll call him right now. Talk to you later."

When I tried to reach Roy, he wasn't there either. I cringed at the message we'd recorded together in New York, the one that ended with him saying into the microphone, "Morgan, now what do I do?" And then there was the beep.

"Daddy, it's me. I need you to do me a favor and fast. Please call me back. Love you, as always, me."

I couldn't believe what I had heard from Gladys. A mother knows her child. Being alone in the house gave me the despicable urge to dig deeper into Peter's past. It was almost four. Gladys and Rain would be back soon. And Zeke would have been back at 6. *Creepy that she was still keeping a dead man's time.* The old wooden desk near the crib had stickers from Peter's high school all over the top. I was surprised that Gladys hadn't gotten rid of it. It was an eyesore. Peter must have convinced her to keep it with those stunning blue eyes of his.

The back of the desk was a corkboard with pictures all over it of Peter and a host of girls from high school. They were all different sizes, shapes, and races. The girls all had innocent smiles and were clearly delighted to be posing with Peter Holmes. I was amused at the thought that I'd married the small-town hero. For me, coming from Eastside Girls Academy, his past had a cartoon-like quality. Peter had been a football star. The photos were of smiling teenagers with their own cars, letter jackets, and pretty girls hanging off their boyfriends like costume jewelry.

I found myself fingering the edge of the desk, desperate to look inside. *Was it invading his privacy when it was old stuff from high school?* I couldn't help myself. I opened the overstuffed drawer and saw a journal. I opened the first page and it was Peter's recognizable scrawl.

Lied to Cindy about being with Michelle on Friday night.

Lied to Coach about being sick when I skipped practice.

Lied to Aunt Gladys about the party when they went away.

Lied to Uncle Zeke about wrecking his car.

Lied about the money for the class ring.

The list went on and on. I had to sit down it was taking so long to get through it. The time flew by and I was annoyed to hear the rumblings of the garage door opening and Gladys' car coming into the garage. I shoved the fragile book back into the drawer and went out to help Gladys with Rain and the groceries.

"Morgan, what's the matter? Is everything okay? You look a little funny, love," Gladys said as I opened the door hurriedly.

"Everything's fine. I spoke to Rene. She got me an appointment with the doctor for next Tuesday afternoon. I was thinking that I would spend the night on Monday and maybe come back on Wednesday or Thursday. I'd leave Rain with you if that's okay."

"That's perfectly fine. She'll have a great time being spoiled by her Gladdy. I'll drive you to Rene's house on Monday, around dinnertime."

"That sounds perfect. Thank you again, Glad," I said hugging her.

I had become an actress too.

CHAPTER 8 | *Out of Bounds*

It was finally Monday and Rene said that she would pick me up from Ladera Heights so that Gladys wouldn't have to drive all the way to West Hollywood. Rene suggested that she come before dinner to avoid rush hour traffic. I was excited to finally meet her and breathe some fresh, not floral, air.

Gladys, as expected, had been a gracious host, feeding Rain and I all of our favorite foods. The days in Ladera Heights had been relaxing and everything in and on my body were improving. I was amazed at how dutifully Gladys donned her color-coded daily corsages and went to the prison to oversee the prison's medical department. She had worked there for many years in senior management. She said that the corsages made her inmates feel hopeful, which was why she insisted on wearing them.

Gladys had taken the day off from work. She had been elected to be the co-chairperson of Pastor Jackson's anniversary ball. She couldn't wait to take Rain to church to show her off. I was in the house alone when Rene rang the doorbell, which chimed a jazzy version of "Away in a Manger."

I was suddenly nervous as I opened the door. "Rene, I'm so glad to finally meet you," I said at first glance.

She had deep ebony skin. Her straightened hair was fully gray except for the dramatic white streak in front of her ear-length bob. She wore a black silk T-shirt that gripped her body and her non-existent breasts. Her crisp white linen pants and make-up-less face completed her no-nonsense image.

When she saw me, she must have been taken aback by my bare face and chaotic dreadlocks. She quickly turned her upward gaze away from my hair and outstretched her toned arms and said, "*Quel surpris*! Great to meet you, Morgan!"

Apparently, I didn't match the "educated" woman profile that Beauregard must have described. Dreadlocks were a no-no for people who looked like Rene, especially those living in the wading pool that is California. I waited for Rene's "go-on-girl" warmth and it came immediately. "Girl, we have so much to talk about. I *do* like your hair," she said, trying to convince herself. "I thought about doing it too, but I knew it wouldn't go over at the firm."

Rene eagerly offered to carry my leather duffle bag to her car, while I juggled my knapsack and laptop and entered J-E-S-U-S into the alarm's key pad to activate it. She walked briskly to her tiny red vintage Jaguar and effortlessly stuffed my bag into the tight back seat. The car was so small that I worried how I would manage to squeeze my shrunken self into the compact bucket seat and un-squeeze it when we reached our destination.

Rene still had not gotten over my hair. "When'd you decide to lock?" She said as she turned the car on.

"I wanted to for years, but never could bring myself to do it," I said. "You know how some people feel about dreadlocks. Especially timid black folks. You know, my hair used to be just like yours. When I was diagnosed, I figured, what the hell. I will be shut-in for a while and no one would see me. I no longer cared what people thought."

"Really," Rene said with not-so-subtle astonishment. "How was your hair like mine?"

"It was actually longer than yours. It cost me a fortune to keep up."

"Don't I know it, girl," said Rene.

"I once read an article in Essence called 'Living the Lye.' The writer actually called barbered short cuts "amputations," I said. "That's when I decided to grow my hair and go natural. Let me read you something else. I carry this poem around with me in my wallet. I got it out of a British magazine and thought it was inspiring. It's called 'My Lock.'"

We had stopped at a traffic light and Rene listened as I began to read from a tattered sheet:

My locks lock me in.

My locks speak for me and to me

They remind me that my history is bigger than my background

They don't suffer amnesia

They keep me down to earth

they un-lock my treasures

lock by lock

The driver of the car behind us honked. Rene looked back to the road and said, "That's good! Where'd you get it? I want a copy."

"I'll make a copy, but then you'll have to lock your hair," I said deadpan.

"We'll see. Maybe I could. I'm established in the firm now," Rene said, her voice trailing off.

The breezy drive from Ladera Heights was magnificent. The perpetual sun of California warmed the leather seats and injected me with new optimism. Rene was an LA strategist, making all of her decisions based on current traffic conditions. Of course her prediction was correct; we had a nearly effortless commute to West Hollywood.

I felt relief to be away from the crumbling of my home life. Rene's cell phone rang. The ringtone was muffled jazz which meant it was a business call. I took the free moments to admire the swaying palm trees which were alive and vibrant, not stagnant and still like the cacti of the desert. I inhaled and exhaled the new air deeply.

When Rene was finished with her call, we were already exiting the freeway. "We're really close to my house," she said.

Rene's house was hidden in an enclave of small but pricey bungalows. The outside was white brick with black cloth awnings over every window. The garage was detached and far at the back of the driveway. She parked in the middle of the driveway to let me out. "I know the car is small," she apologized. "I'll help you out." She put the car in park, came over to my side and gently helped me lift myself out of the bucket seat. She walked me in and left me there while she went to unload the car.

The inside of Rene's house was small but everything in it was pristine. The angular light fixtures, the tables, the leather picture frames, all were chosen with great attention to detail. The result was an eclectic blend of Afro-centric meets WASP. The plush oversized leather sofas were strange but appealing companions to the small conservative tables. The walls were painted in earthy shades of gold and brown and there were African masks on every wall; their faces serious and proud. There were no pictures of anyone in her life. No friends, no vacations, no memories.

I took a seat on one of the sofas and fell into its embrace. I took off my shoes and sighed as if I had come home. Rene opened the back door holding my bag and said, "Mi casa es su casa. I'm really glad that you were able to come and stay with me for a couple of days." I got up, quickly grabbed my shoes and followed Rene down the rich cherry floored hallway. We walked into the spacious guest bedroom and there was a note on the bed from Rene: *Welcome Morgan!* Short and to the point. She placed my bag at the foot of the queen size bed and walked toward the kitchen. She said, "I'll make dinner for us tonight. Tomorrow we'll go out. What would you prefer, chicken or fish?"

"Fish, please."

"Salmon it is. I'll run to the market. Make yourself at home. We can talk over dinner."

My shoes already off, I proceeded to unpack my medicines and arrange them across the top of the dresser in the order that I was supposed to take them. I had made a habit of leaving them out so I wouldn't forget. Sometimes it slipped my mind that they were the reason I was feeling almost good.

Rene prepared a delicious meal of broiled salmon in lemon and dill sauce. She also served green beans with basil and garlic and tiny gourmet corn muffins made with blue corn meal. She had also brought a couple of bottles of wine and as she set the wine glass in front of me, she said, "Live a little. I'm sure you haven't had a glass of wine since your diagnosis." She was right. I worried about mixing meds and alcohol.

"One glass won't hurt you. Take it from me. I'm still standing."

I took the chilled glass from her hand.

I was actually hungry. It had been a while since I'd sat down with such hunger. Rene's dinner was decadent. I savored the sweet floral spice of Riesling, remembering why it was always my favorite wine.

Rene sat down and immediately bowed her head, closed her eyes and mumbled something unintelligible, finishing with a hearty "Amen." I perfunctorily echoed her with my own wimpy "Amen."

"I need to tell you something," said Rene as she spooned some green beans onto her plate. "I know I don't know you very well, but, I feel that we're becoming friends and you should know..."

"Know what?" I said, worried that it would be more disturbing health news.

"I'm telling you this for my own healing."

"Telling me what?"

Rene said, "Did you ever read 'Giovanni's Room'?"

I hadn't. I was torn between pretending that I did and admitting that I didn't. Beauregard had probably boasted about how well-read I was. Unfortunately, EGA didn't teach black authors like James Baldwin. Their endowment fund relied on them pushing the classics, the *European* classics. In college I never got to it, either.

"No, I haven't, but I've heard a lot about it. Perhaps I'll read it now. I've got time."

"It's in the guest room on the bookshelf. Check it out if you get a chance. It's short." Rene took a healthy sip of her wine and continued. "There's a character, a woman in the book. Her name is Helga...Hella...Helen...or something like that, who says the most prophetic thing. 'It does seem difficult to be at the mercy of some gross, unshaven stranger before you can begin to be yourself'."

"That's deep," I said, suddenly saddened by my own stranger who was once the love of my life. Rene took a graceless final swig of wine and got up to open another bottle. I didn't know what Rene was getting at. The quote reminded me of my own alien existence.

Rene interrupted my thoughts. "I sometimes think that I was living a life of not being myself. I think that could be the reason I got sick. I wasn't being honest with myself or anyone else. What I'm trying to say is..." she took an audible breath and then continued, "I'm gay."

"Really? For how long? Were you always?"

"What does 'always' matter? I finally feel like I'm in my own skin. Why do people ask that?" I had irritated Rene.

"I wasn't trying to offend you, I was just asking. Maybe that wasn't the right thing to ask." I looked around my plate for something else to do with my loose mouth.

"Forgive me, Morgan. I didn't mean to be defensive but there are so many different things to deal with when you come out. There are things you have to explain to straight people so they feel comfortable and a whole different script that you need for gay people so they can assess whether your feelings are legit or just a phase. I guess the fear of inauthenticity makes people defensive."

"You're right." I said not knowing what else to say. I took a sip of my wine.

Rene continued, "I think being sick has opened me up to digging deeper into why my body rebelled. I don't blame Russell, my ex-husband. He was a good guy, one of those over-educated black men who most women would kill for. He was a nerd, actually. He was an engineer and he made good money, but I was still never satisfied. I even tried having affairs with sexier men, bad boys, even *white* boys. I was running from the quicksand of marriage. I didn't want to get sucked into a life that would suck the life out of me. None of those other guys ever really satisfied me, either. I only felt satisfied when I stopped looking outward and started looking inside at what I really wanted from myself and another person. It was around that time I was diagnosed. I guess the damn had burst."

I leaned forward. "I, too feel trapped inside of a life that I no longer recognize. As Peter said, 'a life that I didn't sign up for'."

"He really said that? You have to get real with yourself. Women struggle with that," Rene said.

She got up from the table. The plates were empty with only a few droplets of lemon dill sauce left. Rene was clearing the table and loading the dishwasher. Her back was to me as she said, "By coming out, I feel like my load has finally been lifted."

"When did you realize that you were attracted to women?" I poured myself another glass of white wine and refilled Rene's red.

"I guess I had always been. It was not the physical, it was the emotional. I had always felt emotionally connected to women. With men, I always felt uneven. I couldn't be myself because of all the things that women are supposed to do or not supposed to do."

"Is that the load that you are referring to?" I walked over to the sink and leaned against the counter so I could face her.

Rene said with a lush's grin, "Yes. The load is the woman's burden. It's the insistence that in order to be a woman of any value, you are required to have a man. Preferably, a *husband*. And you have to do what he says you should do. But most of us, black women especially, have been taught that any man will do, including a man-child with his pants dangling around his ankles and marbles in his mouth...you know, the ones who can't say an intelligible sentence or the ones with lots of children and no wives to speak of. It's pathetic." Rene laughed and I heard myself laughing too.

I thought of Gladys and what she was taught. That was suddenly a sobering thought. The whole thing was no longer funny.

Rene was on a roll. I went to sit back down at the table. "At birth, being born a female comes with an imposed tax. Once they see what's between our legs – I mean, *not* between our legs – they slap little pink suits on us and set us on our way to find a boy, like it's a matter of life and death. I couldn't do it so I felt lost for most of my life until I finally dropped the load and found myself."

I didn't know how to respond to what Rene was saying. My loss for words was perhaps because what she was saying made too much sense to me. I just shook my head in agreement and took a bigger sip of Riesling.

As she spoke, my mind had already wandered back to Magda, the one friend that I couldn't get enough of in college. Magda wrote letters that used to burn holes in my hands. They were sensuous and sticky. Her letters were like French kisses; deep and long. I snapped out of my memory with the clanking of stemware as Rene set the table with smaller, dessert wine glasses and a small lemon cake.

"What were you thinking about? You were gone for a moment," Rene prodded.

"Nothing really. Women certainly have a lot to deal with. It's hard being who "they" say we should be. Sometimes, it just doesn't fit. If it is true that the majority of black men are criminals, under-educated or emotionally crippled because they didn't have fathers, it puts a lot of pressure on us. If that's true. Maybe it's not, but that's certainly the way it seems. Sometimes, I feel that we are forced to be martyrs – to save face for the whole black race by settling for a man that doesn't inspire us or make us grow. There are too many voices in our heads."

"Think of the women like me who did what we were supposed to do, faking it all along. That self-deception is enough to make you sick," Rene said.

"Maybe we should sleep on it. You and I can't solve all of the woes of women tonight with two bottles of wine in us," I said.

It felt so good to be talking and thinking again with a friend who was interesting and interested in what I had to say, just like Peter was when we first met. Rene joined me at the table.

"Discovering our truth is the gift that disease gives us. Each day you live, you have to take the time to look high and low for yourself underneath the sickness." Rene took our empty glasses to the sink. She turned the dishwasher on and flipped the light switch over the sink. "Goodnight, my friend. We both need our sleep."

I walked down the hallway to the guest room in a wine haze, searching high and low...

The next morning I was awakened by my cell phone. The sun was blaring through Rene's sheer curtains and my knees were stiff but I felt optimistic. I saw Peter's name on my cell phone and hesitated, wondering if I could be civil. I picked up and he said immediately, "G'morning More. Yesterday was a hectic day. How are things with Rene? Is she nice? Are you having a good time?"

"Rene is great and she has a wonderful house, you were right. This time apart will be good for us. I'm going to see Dr. Lazard today."

"Aunt Gladys told me. You know we can't afford that," Peter said.

"Don't worry about it. It won't cost you a thing."

"Except for a man's pride, Morgan, I hate it when you ask other people to pay for things we can't afford."

"Let's not talk about it. I should get up and get ready."

"Let's agree to disagree," said Peter.

"The quicksand of marriage" stuck to my brain like bubble gum; it was thick and impossible to digest. I worried that I agreed with Rene too much.

Rene had laid out some bagels, vegan cream cheese, and smoked salmon for me. Lupians need their Omega-3s. She left a note: *Went to yoga. Will be back at exactly 11 to get you to your appointment. Be ready!* The note sounded more like the Rene I'd first met, the one who answered her phone with her full name instead of "Hello."

I showered quickly in my private bathroom and dried off with the thirsty Ralph Lauren towels that my host had laid out for me.

The lush smelling citrusy body wash made me feel energized, and I couldn't wait to meet Dr. Lazard.

I put on my best discount store apparel. My body had shrunk. It was wishful thinking that someday I would be able to fit my old wardrobe again. I had started wearing discounted clothing, because suddenly it didn't matter. My favorite shoes smelled of fresh leather-look plastic. I was ready to go. I raked my slightly stiff fingers through my untamable hair and waited for Rene to come back. I had stopped wearing makeup since becoming a Lupian. It had been many months. My makeup bag that used to serve as my security blanket had sort of started rotting at the bottom of my bag. The compact lay dry and desperate like a lonely virgin. I only used Vaseline for my wrinkled lips. I had stopped caring whether people found me attractive. Becoming sick and invisible had offered me privacy. I was no longer in the grips of people's primal instincts.

I was in the living room when Rene arrived carrying in a bouquet of sunflowers. "Thank you for breakfast," I said.

"Look what I got for the table. I love fresh flowers in the house. They make such a difference. Let's roll," Rene said.

As we drove through Los Angeles, I was amazed at the abundance of luxury cars whizzing by us. Rene and I were both too thin to be healthy but the perfect weight to be *stylish*. We both wore dark black sunglasses and were speeding in a Jaguar. Rene's Jaguar was one of the finest on the road and she took great pride in it, washing it every morning. I admired the flowing palm trees that framed the freeway as they whizzed by us. I was amused that the stereotypes of Los Angeles were real. Every car we passed in traffic held male model/movie star wannabes and their chesty blonde arm pieces carved from Botox, silicone, and lipstick. Every person in LA was trying to get into show business, and every tree seemed dying to be selected as location.

We pulled off the freeway and onto Pacific Palisades Boulevard, the tree-lined street where Dr. Lazard's office was. I slowly emerged from the bucket seat on my own. She peered at her watch with pursed lips as if she had just sucked a lemon. "I will wait for two and a half hours," Rene said.

I couldn't imagine my appointment being over so quickly. I remembered the four-hour meeting Rene had told me about when we first spoke about Dr. Lazard. "Remember your first time with him? It may take a bit longer than that," I said.

"That isn't always the case." She insisted. "Move it along. I will be out front in exactly two and a half hours."

I sat in the waiting room with the crumpled copies of my bloodwork results that I always carried with me when seeing new doctors.

The middle-aged man who appeared in the waiting room was olive-skinned with a mane of long wavy black hair tied in a ponytail. His rotund body waddled into the office with a confident gait. Only his face was thin and remotely handsome. I could almost tell what he looked like before when he was young and not yet consumed by life.

"Morgan Holmes?" he said as he approached me. "Glad I could squeeze you in. Please thank Rene for referring you. What can I do for you? Rene told me a little about you already."

I handed Dr. Lazard my blood work results. He scanned the crumpled pages quickly and said, "Shit – you were *sick*." I looked at him, startled. But what I presumed was a slip of the tongue turned out to be his way of communicating with his patients. Dr. Lazard made liberal use of four-letter words. "Sugar fucks you up," he said.

Dr. Lazard took my history. It was every bit as exhaustive as Rene had described. My history covered my years at Eastside, Marigold's death on the subway, my love and hate for Roy, the birth of Rain, and my crumbling marriage. Dr. Lazard listened and furiously took notes and then joined me on the couch so he could feel my energy, just like Rene said he would. He asked me to be quiet so he could listen and discover where the vulnerabilities were in my body. "Shit. Relax. Take a nap." He sat next to me with his eyes closed and his hand on my lower back and my wrists. His hands were warm and smooth similar to the boiling heat that was bubbling up inside me.

In assessing my history, Dr. Lazard decided that there had been two big shocks in my life. The first was the loss of Marigold. The second was my dying marriage.

We spent about two hours talking and 30 minutes of him feeling my back and arms. He explained my situation in holistic terms, saying that kidneys hold all of the "shocks." The kidneys purify the blood and retain the toxins generated by physical and emotional trauma. According to him, my kidneys had been hit hard twice over the past two decades and that is why they were irritated.

Being with Dr. Lazard made me feel some things that I had forgotten how to feel. I was suddenly staring at the outline of his lips, which were thin but curvy. I imagined running my fingers through his Mediterranean Afro. I imagined him touching me underneath my bra strap and not being able to stop himself. Suddenly, I was getting hot, not knowing if it was my dormant desire or a typical Lupian low-grade fever.

I looked at the clock. It had been 2 hours and 45 minutes, 15 minutes longer than Rene had agreed to wait. Dr. Lazard wanted to give me some medicines to "strengthen my constitution." It was a tiny $15 bottle of pellets that I was to let melt under my tongue. He said they were included with the initial consultation. Dr. Lazard asked if I could wait 15 more minutes so he could have my pulses checked again to make sure the medicines were working. I looked at my watch. *I had to go.* Rene would be pissed but surely she would understand.

He gave me the sugary pellets and asked me to wait in the waiting room. I looked out the window for Rene's Jaguar. I didn't see it - or her - anywhere. I told the nurse I'd be back and went outside into the LA heat. I looked down the length of the block, as well as in the back parking lot. Rene was not there. I went back in and waited 20 more minutes and eventually Dr. Lazard came out of the back office. He had a mischievous grin on his face as if he had been touching himself.

I tried to compose myself – because just the thought of him behind closed doors made me sweat again. Dr. Lazard invited me back into his office for a last look. I was getting worried about Rene. He took my pulse and said that it had improved in the last 20 minutes and assured me that it was a long-term process and it would probably keep improving for the next 30 days or so. He said I was free to go, but he insisted that I come back for a follow-up two weeks later. I made the $175 appointment, knowing that it would be cancelled. I walked out of his office nearly four hours after I had arrived. There was no vintage Jaguar anywhere on the wide street. I panicked. I looked again. I sat on the curb. I sat in the parking lot. I finally went back inside and called Rene's cell.

Had something happened to Rene? Or was something happening to me, like the sun would set and I would be stuck with no money in Pacific Palisades, California? I called her but she didn't answer. I left a message, trying to sound casual, "Hey Rene. I'm so sorry that my appointment ran so late. Hopefully you went to grab a bite. I'm starving too! Just wanted to tell you I'm ready now. Call me back when you're on your way."

I left the office and waited on the front steps for another 25 minutes before Rene finally called me back. "Morgan, I just got your message. I can't come back for you now. It's just about to be rush hour. It would take hours to get back across town."

"Where are you?" I demanded.

"Nowhere near you. Did you expect me to wait around for over three hours?

I said, "No," although I meant *Yes, dammit!*

I was certain Rene would apologize to me for stranding me and then she would say, "I will be there as soon as I can get there."

Instead, she said, "I waited for 15 extra minutes and then I had to get something to eat."

Why didn't you come back? I pouted silently.

Rene continued, "Actually girl, something happened."

"What?"

"I met someone."

"*What?*" I said enraged.

"I was sitting in a café reading a book and the most beautiful woman with the prettiest smile came up to me and asked me if she could join me."

"Rene, what does that have to do with how I'll get back to West Hollywood tonight? You know I have no money. All I had was the check you gave me for Dr. Lazard. How am I going to get back to your house?"

"How would I know that you had no money?" Rene asked. "I would tell you to take the bus, but the buses are on strike. Here's what I recommend; go across the street to the Pacific Palisades Hilton and ask them to call you a cab. It's pretty simple. My address is 888 Palm Tree Court – West Hollywood. Any cab driver will know where it is. Besides, you're a big girl from New York, you'll get home."

Even in my current dishevelment, I managed to raise up all of my learned EGA arrogance, cross the street and meekly asked the concierge to call me a cab. He said that the dispatcher estimated it would be around $25. It was about 10 miles. *It was far*.

The cab came and I got in boldly, praying the whole way that something miraculous would happen. My cell phone was ringing and

I noticed it was Peter. I ignored it because I had a more immediate crisis. I would call back later, once I was back at Rene's.

We arrived at 888 Palm Tree Court; the driver took my American Express card and started punching numbers into a small electronic console. I said casually, "Are you running the card?" My cell phone rang again. It was Peter. I ignored him, worrying more about what to do if this hot-headed cab driver would not take kindly to me saying that I couldn't pay him.

"Of course, I'm callin' it in. Ya think I'm stupid?" said the driver. His accent was bumpy, his tone annoyed.

I panicked.

"I'm sorry, let me give you another card." I slipped him my well-overdrawn debit card.

Just as he took the overdrawn card, there was a tap at his window. It was Rene. The driver rolled the window down and said without looking at her, "Where are you headed?"

Rene said, "I'm not going anywhere. I want to pay for my friend. How much is it?" She handed him two crisp twenty dollar bills.

I felt tears rolling down my face. I didn't know what to say to Rene. I was torn between "thank you" and "fuck you." I got out of the cab shaken and walked past Rene while she tipped him and retrieved her change. When I got into the house, I didn't want to stand or sit down. I was exhausted, frustrated and regretted that I had come to Los Angeles at all.

Peter was calling again and I ignored him. He could wait.

I opened Rene's refrigerator and found the last gulps of the white wine from the night before. I pulled a water glass out of the cabinet and poured. Rene was right, a little wine wouldn't kill me.

"Morgan, I'm so sorry." She was coming in from outside but she started her apology before she made it in. "At least you did what I suggested. See, it all worked out, right?"

I stood at the doorway to the kitchen, without knowing what to say or how to say it.

"Yes," is all I got out.

"Oh good."

"*No good.* How dare you leave me stranded in the middle of Pacific Palisades? I don't get how lunching with a stranger was more important than being there for me. I'm your friend. That woman is a stranger."

"Don't say that," Rene said as if pleading with fate.

"I have to say something."

"What do you have to say? I paid for the cab, didn't I? That should make it all better."

"I'm sick, Rene! Sicker than you. I'm scared. I've forgotten what it feels like to wake up and not have to forgive some part of my body for nagging me with senseless pain, irritation or swelling. I am tired of meeting new doctors alone week after week. I am sick of being alone."

"You're awfully needy, Morgan," Rene shot back at me.

"I am needy. And when your hands weren't working you were needy, too. That is what happens to the sick—"

"—and, the lonely," said Rene as she fled the kitchen.

From the other room she yelled, "What happened today was a fluke. I've never met someone like that. You just don't understand LA. I don't go to clubs because I can't stand the smoke. It's hard to meet women when you are older. The traffic is horrible here.

Everything and everyone is too far away. I waited for you for two and a half hours, but I couldn't wait any longer."

"But what about me? I needed you today. You could've told that stranger that you could see her later. You could have done lots of other things, but you didn't. You did what people always do; think only of themselves," I screamed.

I could hear Rene's heavy footsteps on the cherry wood floors, coming back into the kitchen. "That's not what people always do, Morgan. I'm a good person. Perhaps I did act selfishly today but I paid for the cab when you said you had no money. Better yet, consider today's appointment a gift. Don't pay me back. Forget it. I'm so sorry for leaving you like that. I have needs, too."

Rene dropped into one of the kitchen chairs cradling her head as she leaned onto the table. Her perfectly coiffed hair fell over her hands. "What else do you want from me?"

I gained my composure, wiped my forming tears away and said, "Nothing else, I guess. I'm sorry for overreacting. Thank you for saying what you said. And, being so generous."

My cell phone rang again. It was Peter again. I walked out of the kitchen to see what happened, if anything at all.

CHAPTER 9 | *Washed Away*

"Hello?" I whispered into the phone.

"Morgan! There was a flood. Everything has been destroyed."

The shrillness of Peter's voice startled me. "What do you mean?"

"A pipe in the dishwasher burst. I wasn't here, but when I got home, there was water everywhere. Everything was floating through the house. Letters, mail that was on the coffee table. Everything's wet. It's a disaster."

"Explain this to me again." I couldn't comprehend. "Are you OK? What did you do after you saw the water?" I asked him.

"I didn't know what to do. I ran over to the Kanes'. They were home and told me what to do. I called a 24-hour water damage company. They came right away. They say the damage is pretty severe. The water had sat for a long time, further weakening the structure of the house and allowing bacteria and mold to start growing. Almost everything in the house has to be removed and thrown out." His voice was breathy with fear.

My knees wobbled as I listened. I looked around Rene's hallway for something to hold onto and noticed the skylight over my head. Its glare made me dizzy. I turned away from the light. *People with Lupus are sensitive to light.*

"What time did you get home?"

"Around 6. When I was calling you and you wouldn't answer the phone. "

"I'm sorry about that. I was dealing with another problem."

"None of that matters. What matters is that everything we have has been destroyed."

I was speechless. I felt the tears coming on. I didn't know what to feel or what to say. I had grown so suspicious of Peter. I never knew what to believe. *This sounded suspicious.*

My hands gripped the phone tighter to absorb my mounting frustration.

"Morgan, say something. You always want to blame someone. You can't blame this on me."

"Did the flood reach Rain's room?"

"Her stuff's gone, too. Her teddy bears are all waterlogged. Her linens, her clothes. They all had to be thrown away."

"That'll break her little heart."

"Your music cabinet collapsed. The water softened the wood. The CDs all fell out and were under the water when I got here. The vinyl records are also gone. The guys from the water company put whatever seemed salvageable in black mold-resistant trash bags. They said you could try to save some of them, but all of the vinyl and most of the CDs are gone."

Dread sucked the wind out of me. Reality had begun to sink in. Horror and a strange sense of relief swept over me.

"More, you still there?"

My heart sank as I said trembling, "I've spent my whole life collecting music..." My voice trailed off as I remembered Marigold and how she got lost in music and how it was her saving grace on those lonely nights when her only companions were vodka, grapefruit juice, and Al Green. I had taken the baton from her.

My mouth was dry. "I'll never be able to replace them all. I never catalogued them. I always meant to, but..."

"We both need to pray for strength."

"Are our clothes ruined, too?" I really didn't care but I needed to say something and nothing more would come.

"That's all that's left is our clothes. They were hanging up so they were not close to the water. The water guy said that we should have them all dry cleaned just to remove any possible mold. The carpet in the closet may have mold."

"I called the insurance company. They're gonna fax me some forms to fill out. We have to list all the things that were lost. I'll take care of it."

I needed to sit down. There was an African leather bench that Rene had placed next to the bookshelf. It was not meant for sitting, but I did anyway.

"I can't take anymore," I said into the phone.

"We have to deal with this. There is no time to have a pity party. Let's just get the lists done now. Hold on, there's someone at the door." While I waited, my mind was blank. I could no longer think. I was at Peter's mercy. He returned to the phone. "It's the blowers. They're here."

"What are the blowers?"

"Huge industrial fans that take away mold and dehumidifiers that reduce the moisture in the air. After that in a couple more days they will bring deodorizers and air sanitizers. It'll take several days to have the house even inhabitable again."

"Rain and I should come back to help."

"No. You don't need to. You can't stay in the house anyway. Even I have to find a place to sleep. The carpets reek of mold. It's a toxic environment. I definitely don't want you or Rain here. It's too dangerous. This company seems pretty good. They know what they're doing.

"Where did you sleep last night and where will you sleep tonight?"

"I was fine. I found a place."

"Where will you sleep over the next few days?"

"Maybe I'll ask Chad and Laura…I'll find a place. Kiss Rain for me. I'm really sorry about all this."

"I'm sorry, too…." *Sorry I don't believe you.*

I started the next day as I always did, although everything in my world was no longer mine. I lay in Rene's guest bed with the sun streaming through the blinds, warming me. I had struggled all night with sleep, without letting Rene know what had happened. The flood seemed so implausible that I was embarrassed to tell her. It could be true. *But it may not be.* I felt sick and relieved at the same time. Peter and I, according to him, no longer had anything. Peter's description of the flood didn't make sense to me.

Distance makes the heart grow harder.

I ran it over in my own head again and again. I was soon-to-be a divorced, single mother with no money and nothing even left to sell. I had lost all of the things that Eastside Girls Academy said an educated woman was entitled to. The room was calm around me. I felt myself smile, then a laugh spilled from my lips. The laugh became louder and louder until Rene knocked on the door. She rattled the knob and barged in wearing her yoga clothes with her yellow mat tucked under her arm.

"What's so funny?" she said as she stood in the doorway.

"That call last night? It was Peter telling me that our house flooded."

"Why didn't you come get me?"

"I was in shock. Nothing like that has ever happened before."

"How did it happen? Was he there?"

"Apparently not. He didn't find it until the evening. The tubing in the dishwasher burst. He was calling me non-stop yesterday, but I was trying to get back from the doctor and didn't talk to him until last night after dinner."

"What did you lose?"

"Lots of stuff that I guess we never needed. He says my music collection is gone. Peter says that the water must have sat for more than 12 hours."

Rene dropped her yoga mat at my feet and sat down on my crumpled sheets as I paced back and forth in front of the bay window. "Peter called the insurance company. He's waiting for an adjuster to come out later today."

"Do you have a home warranty?"

"We let it expire."

"The dishwasher company would have paid you damages if you could prove that it was a malfunction of the dishwasher...Can you prove that it was? Shouldn't you go back to Arizona to take care of this with him?"

"I offered to come back but he said no." I stopped pacing and faced Rene, "I think he's going to ask for a divorce."

"He wouldn't do that now. This is not the time. It could cause a big flare-up for you. The stress will cause everything in your body to start swelling again."

I picked up pacing again. "I can just sense something's up. I somehow don't believe this flood happened. By itself."

"Why a flood? He's going to have to stage a lot to make it even remotely credible for you when you get home."

"That's why he's buying time. That's why he didn't want us to come back. He's just desperate. I can't place my finger on it, but it will all come out soon, whatever it is."

"Please stop pacing, you're wearing out my Berber carpet." Rene stood up to hug me and stop me from pacing. I breathed in the calm of her lavender oil.

"Come to think of it, this all sounds strangely familiar," she said. "I once read something about compulsive liars in a law journal. I worked on a case that involved one. High drama is a part of their strategy. There's always a fire or a flood, a police chase, a trip to the emergency room, or something over-the-top to cover up the foundational lie. The drama covers up and creates sympathy for the liar. It's really quite fascinating."

"The flood just doesn't seem right. I can feel that something's wrong with all of this. "

"Well, I hate to say it, but I don't buy it, either. It seems like a classic case."

"What do you think I should do?"

"Nothing. Let him talk to the adjuster and the insurance company. Let's see what they tell him to do. Let it play itself out. You won't be responsible for any of it. You weren't there and he told you not to come back. That in and of itself is suspicious."

"It is." I wanted to be left alone. I put my hand on Rene's shoulder and said with a slight push, "Go on to yoga. Don't be late for class discussing this mess."

"Wanna come to class? It may help with your stress." *As though I could actually stretch while my life had shriveled and drowned.*

There was suddenly comfort in the certainty of nothingness.

I canceled my follow-up with Dr. Lazard. Roy had overnighted me a check made out to Rene for my initial appointment, but not without scolding me for borrowing money from a stranger and the exorbitant cost of overnight service. When I left the check on Rene's kitchen table, hours later it was ripped into little pieces which she left for me along with a note: *"Like I said, it's a gift."*

The next morning while Rene was at yoga, I took a short walk through her neighborhood. The palm trees on her street seemed friendlier, not so desperate to be seen. Although I had lost over thirty pounds in the last six months, I was slowly starting to gain weight. I was no longer confused about the value of heft. I was no longer the Eastside girl that I once was. My small pants were no longer falling off. I yearned for my thighs to be more ample and my skin to cling to my curves with no excess.

I was due to return to Gladys' to pick up Rain for our trip back to Oro Valley. When Peter told me there was no need for me to come back early, he convinced me that there was no reason to change my flight and pay the penalty that neither of us could afford. I didn't argue. I was as scared to see him as he was to see me.

kim green

CHAPTER 10 | *Cleaning Out*

End of November 2004, Los Angeles, California

The day of my departure from Rene's, I awoke with the pressure of a brick holding my heart from its natural rhythm. My chest felt as tight as a smoker's. I wasn't ready to leave, not because I had become so attached to Rene, but I had become re-attached to myself. I had spent these past weeks thinking and planning. I was headed back to Gladys' just to get Rain so we could head back to Oro Valley for me to spend my final days as Peter's wife in our wet world. I anticipated the rebellion of my frail body. I waited for its bizarre tricks of swelling, stiffening up and aching without notice.

Rene had prepared breakfast. She had plunked down another vase of too-tall sunflowers in the center of the table. I peered through them as she put out small platters with poached eggs, smoked salmon, bagels and some more of that curiously tasty vegan cream cheese.

Once seated, Rene picked up her glass of fresh squeezed orange juice. The glass had left a stubborn morsel of pulp on her top lip. "Morgan, I can't believe our visit is over so soon. I really enjoyed spending time with you and I hope meeting Dr. Lazard was helpful to you. I know how much you've been through."

I couldn't stop staring at the embarrassing morsel of pulp. I stuttered, "Thank you, for everything. I hope things work out with that woman that you met."

Rene smiled and the pulp finally dropped into her lap. "Her name's Bethany. Remember that name. I hope so, too, Morgan. You take care of yourself." She filled in my silence with, "I can't wait to meet your little Rain."

I felt slightly nostalgic about Rene. After the stranding, she did prove that she could be a friend, despite her leaving me. "You'll love Rain. She'll be wide awake when we get there. Gladys said she's been saying Mama and looking for me."

"Things won't be as bad as you think they'll be. You're a lot stronger now. Everyday will get easier. Besides you have a little girl to raise. You have to be strong for her. You have to make her strong. As strong as you."

"When I get back to Arizona, I'll just have to see what's left... and what's been washed away." I let myself dream out loud. "Lately, I've been thinking about moving to Atlanta."

"Really? Why Atlanta?"

"Because I have to go somewhere far away from Peter and the mess that our lives have become," I whispered.

Rene looked at me and said, "Morgan, it's OK. This is hard."

"Atlanta is where my mother was born. Maybe that's why I want to go there. I know that sounds crazy."

"Not at all crazy," Rene assured. "In fact, it makes sense to me. Being as sick as you've been has given you time to put all the pieces together for yourself. On a lighter note, did you know that the A-T-L is like the gay capital of the East? You know I'll definitely come to see you if you end up there." She smiled, mischievously.

"I guess I knew that, but that's not why I'm going. I hear there are some straight people there, too," I teased.

"Who's in Atlanta?" Rene asked.

"My friend, Dorian."

"An old boyfriend?"

"No. He's sort of like the younger brother I never had. I used to work with him in the music business. He manages a recording studio in Atlanta and he sometimes goes on tour with bands as a tour manager. We were really close back in the day."

Rene's eyes shifted outside of the small talk. She gently prodded, "Eat up! It's almost time to get on the road. Morning rush hour has ended and if we're not careful the lunch traffic will start up."

I lingered, pissed that traffic conditions would stand in the way of my last easy moments. Reality was fast approaching and I was scared of future pain. Rene leaned over and hugged me. She said into my ear, "Take care, girl. I'm here if you need me. I mean it." The smell of her lavender lingered and I wanted to hug her longer.

"I know you do. Thanks, Rene, for everything." I said, knowing that there was nothing more she could do for me. My life was all up to me now.

Rene and I drove without conversation to Ladera Heights. My mouth and brain were paralyzed knowing that the demons of disaster and divorce awaited me. Peter hadn't said it. Neither had I. But there was no other place for our marriage to go. I knew Peter too well. I knew what he would and wouldn't be able to say. I knew how desperate he got when his back was against the wall. He has never been honest. He didn't know how to be. I closed my eyes and let the breeze sweep over my upturned face, daring the sunrays to penetrate the thick bluish sunscreen that I was told to wear, rain or shine. *Doctor's orders.*

Rene said, "Morgan do you feel alright?

"I'm fine. I'm just mentally preparing myself for Gladys."

"Don't forget Rain is there, too. That should make it easier." I was deep in thought about what I would say to Roy. How I would broach the topic of leaving Peter and Arizona. Roy would just see it as another financial obligation. I thought about the brief marriage counseling that Peter and I had sought, which Roy had to pay for. Therapy turned out to be a band-aid for a terminal wound. Roy would tell me that I had been stupid to leave New York in the first place. He would say that he wasn't going to pay for another of my expensive mistakes. He would remind me of my pattern; leaving when I couldn't find what I thought I needed and then never finding it. Roy would repeat that Lupus had been all my fault. My head started to hurt.

I said to Rene with my face turned up to the sun, "Will you turn on the radio?"

Rene pushed the up arrow from her steering wheel to increase the volume so the music could better compete with the sound of the California breeze as it whipped around us. With the radio volume up; the sound of Marvin Gaye filled me. The deep dark sound of his funk poured over me like warm water. The thick guitar grooves and his haunting falsetto calmed me. The sound of his voice was a soul memory and my body reacted before I could stop it. My eyes closed while my shoulders bobbed up and down. My fingers were identifying and touching invisible beats. My feet were tapping to the groove. *"Turn up the music, I got the music,"* Marvin sang underneath the remixed classic. Marvin's falsetto clashed with the rapper's gruff voice and their conflict reminded me of my own soul's conundrum. Bitter and sweet.

I was so deeply immersed in the song, I hadn't realized that we had stopped in front of Gladys' house. When I opened my eyes all I could see was Rene staring at me and a car standing still.

"Girl, you're really into your music!"

Slightly embarrassed, I said, "I told you I was in the music business. You know how I am about music."

"Let's go inside so I can meet the famous Rain."

We were standing in front of Gladys' front door adorned with a little miniature crucifix as the door knocker. I took a deep breath and dove into the depths of my bag to find my key. Gladys would have been very offended had I rung the bell as if I were a stranger.

I keyed into the house and the manmade floral scent stung my face like cheap cologne. I hesitated as always and said, "Glad, I'm home and I have Rene with me."

"Come on in, you two!"

I heard Rain saying, "Mama" and Gladys echoing her.

"Mama is home!" Gladys was holding Rain in her arms and she immediately brought her to me. Her heavenly smile filled me with joy and sorrow. I looked at her and said, "Hi my little sweet! Mommy missed you. Have you been a good girl for your Gladdy?"

"Gooood" is all she could say as she reached for me, trying to pull my short wild locks.

"Rain, this is Mommy's friend, Rene," I said, motioning to her.

"Hi Rain," she said, coming close enough to her face to kiss it. "I have heard so much about you!"

Gladys barged in with her usual niceties, "Hello Rene, dear. Thank you so much for taking Morgan to the doctor and allowing her to spend some time with you."

"I have enjoyed having her."

"Rene, have you ever met my Peacock? My Peter, I mean. Morgan's husband?" Gladys said as though she were speaking about her nephew, the football star.

"No, unfortunately, I haven't had the pleasure. But I've heard a lot about him," Rene coughed and cleared her throat.

"Next time Morgan and Peter come back for the holidays, you'll have to meet him." Turning to me, she said, "Morgan, you can't forget. We have to have Rene over for dinner. That would be so nice. Then she can finally meet your better half. I am so sorry my late husband, Zeke, won't meet you. He would have liked that."

Rene didn't know what to do with hearing the wishes of a dead man.

Rene turned her attention to playing with Rain, reaching and cooing at her in a way that I would not have expected. She finally turned to me and said, "She's precious. Sadly, I need to head back to West Hollywood so I don't run into too much traffic. Will you need a ride to the airport when you leave tomorrow?"

Gladys interjected, "No, thank you, dear. I'll take Morgan and Rain to the airport. But thanks for the offer."

"It was nice to meet you, Mrs. Holmes. Hope to see you again."

"Me too, dear," Gladys said, already walking Rain back into the family room.

I walked Rene out. I felt mad that she was leaving me alone with Gladys and all the things that I had worked so hard to forget. "Rene, I can't thank you enough for everything."

She lowered her voice discreetly and said, "You do need luck dealing with her. Girl, stay in touch. "

I started toward Rene to get one last lavender embrace but she was already headed back to her car, ready to speed out of the Ladera Pavilion subdivision. Never, ever to return.

I went back into the house. I needed to talk to Roy. It had been days since we had spoken. He was mad at me. Roy had the idea that I should speak to him every single day. Whenever I tried suggesting a less frequent check-in plan, like every other day, he would curse and rant at me about how ungrateful I was and how I'd cry when he was dead. He believed strongly that it was a daughter's duty to speak to her "only" father daily. I dreaded the lecture that constantly ran like a pre-recorded tape in my mind. I decided to postpone it. I put my bag back into the guest room and went into the family room where Gladys and Rain were. Gladys was reading the Bible while Rain played with a new noisemaking toy that I didn't recognize. On the TV were four grown men in colorful T-shirts that read "The Wiggles." They were doing a silly dance with their knees and feet flying around the stage – the sort of dances that I hadn't in her lifetime had the energy to do. Rain was enthralled at the sight of big people acting small.

Gladys looked up, "Did you have a nice time with your friend, Morgan? How was the doctor's appointment?"

"Expensive," I said.

"Was he able to help?"

"He helped me understand some important things about my body. I'll tell you about them later."

Gladys insisted, "You don't need that doctor or any doctor or all those pills that you take. I told you the Lord is going to heal you. You just wait."

"I guess Peter told you about the flood."

"Yes, Dear, he told me. I'm so sorry. I've been praying about it ever since. But the Lord told me to look at the good news. God worked it out because neither you nor Rain were there. You have to see how God works. He's amazing, isn't He?"

"Yes He is. How are things going with the Pastor's anniversary planning?" I said.

"Just fine. It's going to be a pleasant evening. It won't be perfect, but it will be good enough."

"What does that mean?" I asked her, keeping my eye on Rain and The Wiggles.

"Well, you know how church people can be. Sometimes they focus on the wrong things, like letting Sister Betty's grandson play the piano when he has only had four lessons or making Sister Lula's granddaughter be the host of the show even though she has a terrible lisp. These church events can get so chaotic. Some people are just not capable of putting on an event that is, you know, elegant."

"So why are you even involved with it?"

I could see out of my eye that Rain had made her way over to the television and was getting dangerously close. I imagined all of Gladys' remotes falling onto Rain's head. I rushed over to her and put her on my lap.

"Morgan, I could never do that. It's my duty to serve the Lord wherever He needs me."

With Rain on my lap, she had managed to place her fingers in my mouth. I spoke through them, trying hard not to bite her. "Why don't you tell them how you feel? Maybe you can show them how to do things the right way."

"I couldn't do that. That would hurt someone's feelings and cause a fuss. You know, start a 'she-said, he-said' war. Don't you repeat what I've said about any of this. This is just between you and me." She caressed my cheek.

"I promise."

"You know, Morgan, when Peacock was about ten years old, he'd always pull me aside after church and say, 'Aunt Gladys, why did you tell that woman that her hair looked good when it didn't or that her dress was pretty when it was ugly? Isn't that lying?' he would ask. My Peacock has such unusual blue eyes...I would look into those dreamy eyes and tell him that it wasn't lying. It was making people feel good, which is more important than always telling the hurtful truth. Don't you agree, Morgan?"

I thought of Marigold and her words tumbled out of my mouth as if they were my own. *"'If you'll lie, you'll steal and if you'll steal you'll kill.'* That's what my mother taught me."

"Well, isn't that a *different* approach? That seems a little harsh to teach a child," Gladys said scornfully.

"Parents of only children tend to raise them a little tougher. I guess that's because they think they only have one shot."

"That's exactly why you and Peacock need to get Rain a little sister or brother right away. Only children seem to have it so much harder than other children."

"Yes. Yes, we do."

Gladys suggested I arrange wheelchair service again, but I felt like I could make it this time as long as she carried Rain and our luggage was on a cart that I could push and lean on for stability in case I felt tired. I was strong enough to try to walk through LAX and the small Tucson airport, which was closest to Oro Valley. Gladys, Rain, and I all did our wet goodbyes with Gladys' tears and Rain's saliva binding the ceremony. Gladys whispered slyly, "Keep our secrets, please, dear."

I hugged her tightly and said, "I promise."

Peter was standing behind the velvet rope. As I approached him, butterflies swirled inside my stomach. I felt as if I were meeting a blind date, although so much of me had been an integral part of him for nearly ten years. It was strange seeing him as someone who was no longer attached to me. He was like a lost appendage; so painfully familiar but separate. As I got closer, I noticed that he was on his cell phone and when he saw me, he quickly shoved it into his shirt pocket.

With his arms outstretched, he said playfully, "Hey Rain!" He hesitated and then added, "Welcome home, Morgan." Peter grabbed our daughter out of my hands and showered her with love and kisses. Jealousy arose in me again.

"You have gotten so big!" he said to her, as if I weren't even there to agree. "How many bags do you have? You know I'm on my lunch break. Let's make it quick."

"How's the house?" I asked flatly.

"It's OK. There are fans and blowers all over the house. The mold specialist came and said he'd have to wait until the carpets dried to remove them. The house smells terrible. It won't be a good environment for Rain. Or you, for that matter.

"Two bags," I answered.

We walked in silence to baggage claim, with the only sound being Rain's attempts at words that were still too large to live and breathe in her tiny mouth. Peter and I were both desperate to say something but neither of us had words that would fit.

Peter's phone rang again and he looked nervously at it and silenced it.

"Who was that?"

Peter ignored the question as the bags finally came around the carousel.

We drove quietly. Rain had just started using a sippy cup and was spilling red juice all over her yellow T-shirt. Peter was lost in thought. For once, he wasn't worrying about his tan leather seats. I peered out of the window at the bizarre beauty of the desert. It was like a black-and-white photo of a former life.

I abhorred the weightiness of our silence, so I said something that I shouldn't have. "You still didn't ask me how my trip was."

"Morgan, I just talked to you. I know how your trip was. You already said that you liked Rene and that her house was nice and comfortable and that Aunt Gladys took great care of you and Rain. Oh yeah, I forgot to ask how was that quack doctor that you were so excited about?"

We had arrived at our stucco two story house that had looked just like I dreamed it would, when I was still a dreamer. Peter popped the trunk from inside and ran around the car to open my door for me. With strain in his voice from lifting my heavy bag, he said, "Did he cure you?"

"Do I look cured? Since you did so much research, you should know there's no cure. He was too expensive for me to even get close to a cure. But at least I got a holistic perspective."

"I told you, you couldn't afford it," Peter said as he opened the door and the musty smell greeted me, turning my stomach.

"It smells terrible in here."

"Told you."

"You won't be able to stay here tonight. For even a couple of hours. I talked to the Kanes' next door. They said they would be happy for you and Rain to stay with them for the next couple of days. You can just walk over there when you are ready. You shouldn't keep Rain in here for too long."

"Are you coming back after work? Where will you stay tonight?"

"I'm covered. I'll call you later. Be careful in here. Mrs. Kane is expecting you any time now."

As he walked toward the door, I said to his back, "In sickness and in health."

The quicksand of marriage had sucked me in. I was turning into an attacking wife who was being attacked by her own body. Peter wouldn't be returning that night, I knew. He said he had a place to stay. I was too tired to pry.

I remembered the words of Dr. Fair, our marriage counselor, "If you choose to separate, you no longer have the right to question Peter's actions. Your expectations should no longer be those of a wife."

I stood in the center of the house. The blowers were loud and hard at work sucking the moisture out of the room. Rain didn't like the sound of them. I held her in my arms so that she wouldn't get a finger stuck in something.

I walked through the house and my shoes made a sound as they sloshed through the remaining puddles. It was awkward to be back there, the stranger that I had become.

I drifted from room to room with Rain who looked startled at our dismantled house. I shivered at the thought of how a random technological malfunction could change a whole life. The black anti-mold bags were everywhere, stuffed with our wet belongings. Instead of trying to salvage anything, I said my silent goodbyes. The art on the walls from all of our travels remained mounted. The framed photos had already developed some evidence of gray mold on the frames. We could wipe them off. They could be saved, but there was no need. They were trash like everything else.

I peered out the back window from the master bedroom at the pool that had gone green from neglect. I looked at the green water with pity, like a mother looking at an expensive toy that had gone un-played with. The pool was simply for status. Neither of us could swim. I looked longingly at the Jacuzzi, remembering all the New Year's Eve celebrations where it had been our tradition to drink champagne and toast each New Year with visiting friends, celebrating how far we had all come.

I didn't know where to start, throwing away everything that in another lifetime, meant so much. I was anxious to rid myself of this pain and evidence. This purging had to be done alone. I decided to walk Rain next door to the Kanes'. Mrs. Kane would be genuinely happy to see us again.

I approached the big wall unit in the living room. It leaned to one side, the shelves were bare. The water people must have pulled everything off the shelves and put them in anti-mold black bags. They must have enjoyed the stories of our past through pictures of better days and friends long gone. They must have marveled at Peter's football days and the array of old girlfriends he had collected.

My box of letters from Magda remained on the top shelf where I had left it. The shelf was buckling from the moisture but the paper lining of the box had wrinkled, but survived. I had carried those letters with me through the decades. They had traveled across the country like precious jewels. I was tempted to relive those moments of youth and shameless infatuation, but I thought better of it, not wanting to bear the weight of regret. Those letters held who I was, not who I had become. I was tempted to read one but I knew it would make me too sad. I looked at the box again, holding it in my hand. It was to be opened at another time when there was enough time to remember.

I had spent too much time in the toxic environment. There was really nothing more to look at. I took all of the paintings off the walls and threw them in large boxes that the water people had left. The art was not particularly fine, it was just fine because we bought it together. It was no longer of any value to either one of us.

It was time to join Rain at the Kanes' and settle in to a couple of days pretending that the Holmes Family was still intact. When I walked up to the front door, Rain was sitting on Mrs. Kane's lap holding a sippy cup full of lemonade.

"Morgan, how did the house look? I'm so sorry you had to come back to all of this. It's the darndest thing how these things happen. How was your trip? Peter mentioned that you were feeling a little under the weather. Are you feeling better? He said you just needed some R&R. Before I forget, while you were both away, your mail was overflowing so I took the liberty to take it in for you. I left it all in the guest room where you and Rain will be staying. Peter said that he'd be staying with another friend since we only have a small guest room. So sorry we can't accommodate you all."

"That's fine Mrs. Kane. Thank you for getting our mail." *Peter hadn't mentioned that he was away.*

"The guest room is just left of the bathroom. Make yourself at home. The mail is on the dresser."

My mail these days consisted of unpaid doctor bills, lab bills and fliers from medical supply stores. There were fliers for wheelchairs, dialysis services, and sales on canes. It was all garbage and although some of it was of relevance to me, I refused to look at any of it. I saw the mail that Mrs. Kane referred to on the dresser. The letters were bound with a red thick rubber band. I sifted through it. Bills, bills, appointment reminder postcards, a coupon for a visual field test from my eye doctor, and a letter. The handwriting was unfamiliar. The EGA girls all had the same handwriting. We had all learned cursive writing in the 4th grade. Our writing style was all the same. This letter was handwritten with no return address. It was addressed to More Holmes. Only Peter called me More.

CHAPTER 11 | *A Place to Put the Pain*

Oro Valley, Arizona, December, 2004

D*ear More,*

I am sure that this letter will come as a surprise to you. I am nervous as I write, but I realize that the contents of this letter must be known to you. Peter has kept you in the dark for too long.

You must have wondered where he goes on the weekends. Where he takes Rain when he's supposedly giving you a break. I know he told you something that you easily believed, because Peter is good at that. He tells people what they want to hear. I tell people what they need to hear.

Peter and I come from the same Parish in Jamaica. We both were sent away for a better life in the states when we were young. Peter and me have a very special connection that I know you'll never understand. The circumstances of our coming to the states are quite different, but the fact that we are here, brings us together in a deep way.

Peter is not a perfect man. He tries to please everyone and never really pleases anyone. I can't go on loving him the way I do knowing that you are still in his heart somewhere.

I know that things have changed with your illness and all. I know you are trying to get well, but you should know that Peter loves me. He is gone. He has moved on. Once all of us understand this, we can all begin to heal. Too many secrets do no good.

Peter and I are both of God. God would not want us to hurt you anymore with all these secrets and lies. He doesn't want me to be a mistress for the man that I truly love and who truly loves me.

Peter and I want to respect you as much as we can under the circumstances. But it's time for you to respect Peter's choice. I am sincerely sorry. I know that you are going through a lot.

How shall I end this letter? Is it goodbye or hello?

Will I ever see you again? Will Peter keep you away from me because he is afraid of what you may do to me? Will he and I eventually be forced to turn our backs on you in your time of need? Or will we all try to get along in respect for our precious Rain?

It's all in your hands now, now that you know.

Respectfully,

Veloris Sangster

I couldn't breathe. With shaking hands, I tried to ball up the pages, but then I realized that I would need them as evidence. Knowing Peter, he would say, "It's not what you think." Hot tears stung my eyes and my throat ached with the screams I suppressed because I was in someone else's home.

I picked up my cell phone and forgot what to do with it. The deafening dial tone sounded angry. I reached for the familiar. I called Roy.

"Hello?"

My voice shook; all I could say was "Help me."

"Morgan? What happened! Where are you?"

"I received a letter from her. I knew it. He's been cheating. He's a liar!"

As always when Roy was enraged, he turned cruel. "A letter from who? What do ya expect me to do? I haven't heard from you in days. Where've you been? Why haven't you called me?"

"Daddy, I need you. I need your help! I don't know what to do. It's hurts so much."

I was sitting in the corner of Mrs. Kane's cramped guest room. I had to get myself together. I didn't want Rain to see her mother in pieces. I had crumpled myself into a ball in the corner.

Roy raged on, "You always need me and that's the only time you call."

Calling Roy was a mistake.

"Daddy, please listen to me. For once. Please care about what's happening now. I've been busy, trying to decide what I'm going to do. I could *feel* this was going to happen. I knew it!"

"Morgan, you always come to me to rescue you but you never take a minute to see how I'm doing. I'm damned 78 years old. What about me? It's not all about you."

The sudden anger I felt stirred me. "You always do this. I can't handle you."

I could barely hear him saying, "I can't handle you, either!" as the phone sailed across the room.

My cell phone rang again. It was Roy. I didn't want to talk to him. I hated him for being who he had always been: brutal and harsh.

I closed my eyes and prayed to Gladys' God; the God who makes miracles happen. The God who sees everything and rights everything that's wrong. The God that I hadn't believed in since I was 15 years old.

God, help me. I am in pain. Lord, help me make the right decision about what to do and where to go. Help me out. Give me the strength to take Rain and give her the life that we promised her. God put strength back into my body.

Every word I prayed made me feel better. My heart was no longer racing. I was able to walk to the front of Mrs. Kane's house. I was able to smile and tell her mild stories of my relaxing time away. I was able to hold Rain on my lap bouncing her with a nervous rhythm. I was in a daze, but I was functioning.

"Are you OK, Morgan?" Mrs. Kane asked.

"Why do you ask? I'm fine."

"You look a little shaken."

"I'm fine. Better than I was, in fact."

Time had slowed.

My cell phone rang again. I excused myself from Mrs. Kane's porch. I went back into the guest room without Rain.

"Ava, it's me," Roy spoke first. His voice was slow and careful, as though there were glass on his tongue.

"I know," I said, resigned to do the father/daughter dance that we always did.

"Ava, listen. You know I love you with all my heart. You know I would do anything for you. I'm sorry for what I said. It wasn't the right time."

"It never is, Daddy."

"I get so mad when I don't hear from you. You know you are my life. I'm sorry that Peter's doing what he's doing. I know how much that hurts."

"How do you know?"

He took a deep breath and as if he was spitting out the glass he said, "Ya Mama did it to me."

But you used to hit her. Instead I said, "She did?"

I was shocked, but I understood without knowing the details. Marigold died before she could ever tell me about herself as a woman or as Daddy's wife. She never told me about Daddy's crippling grip and how his fist felt on her face. Daddy had never mentioned it until it was my turn to understand what he had always tried to convey to me: *You can't trust people no matter what they say.* Like him, I, too had a heart that was dashed and dazed. *Now we both would have an excuse to be who life made us: unreasonable, erratic, and enraged. We were damaged.*

"Hold on, baby. Don't worry about killin' that bastard, 'cause I'm going to do it myself." Roy held the phone while I sank to the floor. He could hear me crying quietly into the phone. Silent spasms surged through my body. I feared I was having a seizure, another Lupian adventure. I could feel my head heating up with fever. All I could see in front of my eyes were white streaks. *Stress is the culprit.*

Roy broke the silence. "What do you need me to do?" Roy's voice was quieter and calm. He had been weakened by the torrent of my pain.

"Just get me out of here. Please help us. Rain and I need to leave. We have to get away."

"How dare Peter do this to you? After you've been so damned good to him. I knew he would do this to you. You gave him too much, too soon. He was totally undeserving of what you did for his ass. Where's the asshole now?"

"Work. We're not at home. The house flooded while we were gone. Rain and I are at our neighbors'. Peter, I'm sure will stay with *her*."

"Besides the neighbors who do you have in Oro Valley that you could go to tonight?"

"Nobody," I said, too tired to discern between friends and foes.

"How can that be? You said that you made some friends out there," Roy said, straining to be gentle.

"I did and there's nobody I'd want to humiliate myself in front of." I could imagine the people that I worked with at the recording studio who could not do a thing for me. This was my personal hell.

"Believe me, Ava, all those people have already gone through this shit. I hate to say it but people are treacherous. They can't help themselves."

"Daddy, I'm thinking of going to Atlanta."

"Why don't you come back to New York? You and Rain could live here until you get yourself back on your feet," he said, hopefully.

I shuddered at the thought of returning to old dirt. "I want to go to Atlanta. Dorian lives there."

"Why would you go there when you have a home in New York? What's going on with you and Dorian, anyway?" he asked; always the accuser.

"Nothing. He's a good friend and he travels all the time on tours. He has a house that Rain and I can stay in until I figure things out."

"Ava, you haven't figured anything out in all these years. Why don't you let me help you? Your figurin' is what got you into all this shit. I think you should come home. What the hell is in Atlanta, anyway?"

After what Roy had just revealed, I didn't want to further upset him with my need to get closer to Marigold. He pressed me again. "Why Atlanta? Tell me, Ava. Why damned Atlanta?"

"Because that's where mom was born. I just need to get back to the beginning."

It was nearly 10 pm. Roy and I talked for a long time and we ended the conversation with a plan that we both could live with. We were both exhausted. We were satisfied that I would get away from Peter, out of Oro Valley, and a lot closer to New York.

Rain was asleep on my lap in Mrs. Kane's full guest bed. Roy and I had designed a new single mother's life that neither Rain nor I were prepared for. I could have put her down, but I didn't want to. Clinging to her felt right and wrong. I clung to her like Daddy clung to me. *Our offspring become our shield.* The Oro Valley sun had set in a blaze of glory. I would miss it when this chapter of my life was all over. My lap was numb with Rain's dead weight. I called Peter. I was ready to face him. *It was time to fly again.*

I reached for the phone and dialed his number. It went right to voice mail. I hit re-dial.

He picked up, though not immediately. "Hello?"

"Hello. How are you?" I said in a tone imitating calm.

"Is everything all right?"

"Why would there be something wrong?" I said with weak sarcasm.

"You just sound…funny," he said.

"Where are you?" I pressed, ignoring Dr. Fair's instructions on soon-to-be-ex-wife behavior.

"Where did I say I'd be?"

"It sounds awfully quiet."

"I went outside," he said, sensing my thinly veiled suspicion. "What's up?"

"I think you should come home."

"Where will I sleep? You see how small the Kanes' place is."

"You can sleep on their couch."

"I can't do that," he said.

"Okay." I gave in because it would be the last time. "Goodnight, Peter. Sleep well."

I clicked the off button and called Dorian on speed dial. I didn't want Rain and I to be alone with my rage in Mrs. Kane's house.

"Wassup Morgan?"

I told Dorian about Veloris' letter. After only a few lines, he stopped me. "Don't read anymore. I don't want to hear anymore. She's bold as hell. And he's a dumbass. What do you need me to do, Morgan? You know you're always welcome here. Me and my family are here to help. I'm so sorry to hear this."

"I talked to Roy. He said he would help get me out of here."

"You and Rain can come and stay with me until things calm down. Morgan you know you're like my sister. I've got your back. Ya boy, Peter, is a total fuck-up. I'll hit you back soon. The group is on the other phone. Later." And he was gone. *Help was on the way.*

The next morning, Peter showed up at the Kanes'.

Mrs. Kane, unsuspecting, led him into the guest room where his family was. As he stepped inside the door, he asked, "What's wrong, More?"

He looked down at a sleeping Rain and knelt down to kiss her cheek. He got close enough to kiss her and too close to me. His linen shirt reeked of drugstore perfume, the fumes irritating my sensitive skin. I winced at the stench of the letter writer.

I glanced at the clock and my heart was in perfect sync with the ticking of the second hand. He had come before work. It was only 6am. I was nervous seeing him. *I was ready.* I kept my fingers on the tattered letter on the nightstand.

Gladys once told me that the Bible says the only time divorce is acceptable is when there has been adultery. When Peter walked into that room our paths could finally uncross. *I was free at last.*

"What's the matter?"

"I got a letter from someone who seems to know you far better than I do."

"Excuse me? Who would that be?"

Rain was deep in sleep. I smothered her in kisses. "Look," I said as I handed him the letter and stood back from him, not knowing what he would do.

"What the hell?" he said as he took the letter from my shaking hand. Peter's brow was moist. His pale skin had turned ashen. He turned his back to me. He walked in slow motion to the side of the small bed.

"Is it true?" I whispered.

"I need some time. You can't come to me with all this and expect to discuss it now."

"Your time is up."

"I don't want to talk about this now," Peter said, scratching at his familiar door to procrastination.

I stared blankly at Peter, waiting for something. *Anything.*

I repeated, *"Is it all true – the things that she wrote?"*

"Yes," he whispered.

"Is it true?" I repeated, needing further, louder, confirmation.

"YES. IT'S TRUE!"

"Is everything OK in there?" Mrs. Kane said through the door.

"No. But it will be, Mrs. Kane. Please give us a minute."

"No problem. Let me know if you need anything." We waited until she was out of earshot.

My heart filled my throat, then leapt out of my mouth. I imagined it falling to the floor like a crimson-soaked rag. I stared at the invisible mess. I wanted to cry and beg for it not to be true. My throat ached. *The dryness that you are experiencing is called Sjogren's Syndrome, common in Lupus patients.*

I could hear Roy: "You've been too damned nice to Peter. He wasn't worth it." I could hear my Aunt Perris from her Wisconsin grave, "We expected so much more for you, Ava."

I couldn't hear Marigold. She had nothing to say.

"How dare you take our *daughter* into your filth! That was totally out of the bounds of decency. *No one takes their children to their affairs.* How could you be so idiotic?"

"You're right. I'm so *sorry*. I'm sorry. I'm sorry. How many times can I say it?" His head hung low.

"Not nearly enough times to make it disappear."

"What do you want me to do? Kill myself?"

I thought about that for a moment. Peter killing himself would be a blessing. It would do all the things that would make me feel better. It would demonstrate his understanding of the gravity of his sin. And it would remove him from my sight, permanently. I pondered and answered with intentional silence.

He pushed further. "Should I just blow my brains out?"

"If you think that will make you feel better, do it. However, I don't think Rain would be happy about it. But for me, it wouldn't make a bit of difference."

"Well, I have thought about Rain and all you'd have to do is tell her that her father died for his own sins. Tell her that I loved her and left her money. Rain will go on. She has you."

"Shhhhh...she can hear you," I reminded.

It was happening again. Peter was dragging me into that place that he takes me when he is steering me off the path of the issue at hand. He was taking me into all those irrelevant places where we lose the core of the conversation. This had been his game for years. Whenever he was in a jam, he forced us to roam off the road into the oblivion of his personal nonsense. That had always been an ineffable frustration. This feeling would return in future struggles with driving in Atlanta, desperately trying to navigate the circular Interstate 285, which promised to be North/South on the sign and once I entered, the signs read East/West. I would be reminded again of this sinking feeling of thinking you're looking for a specific street but all the streets have the same name. It's thinking you're going one way and actually going another. It would remind me of the rush of blood in my brain that causes vertigo. It is the dread of going further into error at top speed. I would remember this moment whenever I would find myself crying and laughing at the unreasonableness of it all. I would never forget how lost I was with Peter.

My head hurt from Peter taking us around the bend again. I couldn't participate anymore. *Game over.*

"We're leaving. Moving to Atlanta. When I'm not so angry, we can talk about the details. I will never heal in this hellish heat. You need to work it out on your own. You deserve to be in the heat. Not me."

"Please don't take Rain away."

"You can't raise a child when you are one."

My husband and I just sat and listened to each other's shallow breaths as if we were waiting for the fire department to come and rescue us. We were burning.

When I awoke the next morning, the sun was intense, permeating brick and mortar. The heat stole my appetite; all I was hungry for was escape. Rain stayed with Mrs. Kane while I went to get my blood drawn.

I skipped breakfast, only taking my little white Plaquenil pill with a glass of diluted orange juice to cut down the sugar. I stepped into the oppressive and deceitfully cheerful sun. The heat of Arizona felt like the breath of the devil. I got into the car and was already sweating. I removed the foil windshield protector and immediately blasted the air conditioner that took an eternity to cool. *I wanted music*. The CD that I had left in my car before I left for Los Angeles came on immediately as the car started. Dorian had turned me on to the British singer Omar years before in New York. His anthem, "Music," filled my ears. I turned Omar up too loud, remembering the days when Roy would storm around the house screaming "Turn it down, dammit!" I sang the simple hook to myself, "*Mu-ooh-oosic... what I live for.*"

I drove out of the foothills to the flat bland brown landscape that was the city of Oro Valley. I had once seen it as lush and exotic. That was then, when I was in love with the future which promised a husband, a family, and a happy ending. I could suddenly see the starkness and loneliness of the wise and elderly saguaros which had stood alone for centuries, angry and stubborn. The heat no longer warmed, but burned my skin. I sang louder, tears falling from my swollen eyes.

The last time I went to get blood drawn, there had been three phlebotomists taking turns trying to pinch my precious blood out of my stingy veins. They had all walked away, shaking their heads, lamenting, "Her veins are so small." This day was different. They all knew me and were amazed at the plumpness and health of my veins. It was a seven-minute appointment. Only one phlebotomist. And this time it didn't hurt.

Before going back to Mrs. Kane, I turned on the air conditioner and called Dorian. Dorian's rock band had had a hit single called, "F*ck the Madness," which had sold over three million copies. They were touring New York, Los Angeles, DC, Chicago, and then they were off to Eastern Europe for a month.

He answered cheerfully, "Wassup Morgan?"

"What's up with you?"

"Don't you think that Peter will have a fit about you taking Rain out of the state? Are you sure you want to leave so soon? I looked online and there are some complications with taking a child out of state against the will of one of the parents. Did you know about that?"

"Peter will pretend to have a fit, but I know he will actually be relieved. It gives him more time with his mistress."

"Gimme a break, he has a child to think of," Dorian said.

"He obviously wasn't thinking of Rain when he was taking her to be with that bi—"

"—How do you know so much about her, anyway?"

"It's all in that disgusting letter that you stopped me from reading to you."

"You really think Peter will give Rain up that easily?"

"I'm not taking Rain away from him. He's welcome to see her anytime he wants. I just can't stay here in hell. Lupus has been a test for us. Peter failed miserably. I need to pass this test. I need to know what I'm made of. It's not what Peter did or didn't do. It's his instincts which show that he can't be trusted."

"You said you sensed something. You had already planned to leave before you received the letter, right?"

"Sensing and knowing are very different things."

Dr. Tron walked into the exam room with my blood results in his hand. "What did you do?" he asked.

"I just got away for a while," I said. *I laid my burden down. I left the pain, the pregnant pauses, and deafening silences. I left the dinners alone in front of the TV.*

Not one for superlatives, Dr. Tron said, "These blood results are encouraging. I look forward to calling Dr. White and Dr. Valdez. Your white blood cells are up and so are your red blood counts. Your anemia is considerably better. Your kidney function actually looks normal. Your progress is better than most considering how sick you were."

Looking around the sterile office, I nervously cleared my throat and said to his back, "Dr. Tron, do you know of any nephrologists in Atlanta that you could refer me to?"

"Why do you ask? Your kidneys are stable right now, you're free to travel some more, if you'd like. You won't need to see me again for three months."

As he turned back to face me he said, "You *are* coming back, aren't you?"

The answer just hung in the air like a spider web you never notice till you feel it touching your face.

CHAPTER 12 | *Tangling*

Oro Valley, Arizona January 2005

"**M**organ, I've been thinking. I considered flying out there and driving you and Rain back, but it's kinda awkward for me to come into Peter's house and take his wife and daughter away – you know that's foul. Kinda fucked up. I don't want to get into the middle of that shit." The cell phone pressed to my ear emanated heat and too much wattage. "You and Peter were my favorite couple back-in-the-day. I was actually kinda cool with Peter, too, remember?"

"Did I tell you, we don't have a house. The house got flooded when I was away. Peter wasn't staying at the house while I was away, unbeknownst to me. He was with her. So when he discovered the flood it was much worse than it had to be. We are staying with the neighbors. He's staying with her, I guess."

"Morgan, that sucks! It's got to get better for you. No one person can take this much stress."

"Yes they can and we call it Lupus."

"Well, I'm here to help. I thought it would be better if you guys could fly here and I'd just meet you at the airport."

"That would work," I said very slowly. "I understand."

"Don't get me wrong, Morgan. I do want to help – you're like a sister to me. I just don't want to get caught out there – you know what I'm sayin'..." Dorian's voice trailed off.

"You've been hanging around with too many rockstar types." I teased him to eradicate his anxiety and my deep disappointment. My jealous nature rattled. *How dare he think of respecting Peter? He's my friend, dammit.* My friend-greed flared up, a remnant of my girlish EGA past. *Girls fighting tooth and nail for each other's allegiance and affection.*

"I get it, Dorian," I finally said. "It's a fucked-up situation. I'm all fucked-up. My father's right. I never seem to know what I want."

Dorian said, "Nobody knows what they want all of the time. You sometimes end up having to want what you get."

"Am I wrong to not want what *I got?*"

"You're not wrong. You're just coming alive."

"Morgan, how're you? Did you talk to the asshole about the damned letter?" Roy said.

"Yes. It's true. I told him we're leaving."
"What did he say about you taking Rain away?"

"What could he say? He can no longer have the expectations of a married person. That's what that doctor you paid for told us."

"I could have told you that for free."

All I had to bring to Atlanta was Rain and a suitcase full of ill-fitting clothes. Our departure was planned for three weeks. As the day came closer, I started to feel nerves swirling around in my stomach.

I had become my own greatest fear: a poor single mother sleeping in a borrowed bed on borrowed time.

My memories of Georgia sustained me. The red dirt had called me back. I would finally be returning to memories of summers past and the place where my mother was born. Atlanta reminded me of summers with my grandmother, Biggs, and our travels on the Greyhound bus from Wisconsin to Georgia to visit Aunt Robby. The visit always meant a traveling feast. It was always the same; freshly fried chicken wrapped in thick paper towels to soak up the grease. The chicken was always so carefully wrapped in aluminum foil like a shiny Christmas gift. The gooey Wonderbread softened under the chicken's heat. The beige cloth tote bag wore the stains that signified our annual voyage. Ice cold grape soda was our wine. Our dessert was always Biggs's freshly baked coconut cake. By the time the bus pulled into Georgia, 33 hours later, there were only shreds of sweet coconut left on our lips and in our laps, and lots of crumpled foil at our feet.

When I arrive in Atlanta, I will be back in the safety of my grandmother's lap. On the evening of my arrival, I will wait for nightfall and the sound of electric cicadas. I will sniff the sweet perfume of Georgia rains which will wash away my biggest sin; loving him too much and not loving myself enough.

kim green

PART THREE

CHAPTER 13 | *Rising*

Atlanta, Georgia March, 2005

Peter and I are no longer speaking. It's been three months of silence and freedom. There was nothing more for us to say. The time had come for us to retreat to our corners to justify why we did what we did, to each other and to ourselves.

Dorian worried that I was depressed. I was, but not then, when he thought I was. I was just occupied with thinking, straining, and working to reach some kind of peace. It had been a long time. I often sat staring out of Dorian's windows trying to make sense of a life that seemed to have gone off the tracks so violently. I would sit and envision Peter with his head buried deeply in the bosom of his mistress; her making promises that she couldn't keep, while he drank her in thirstily, like a stray desert dog. He no longer called us because he was too ashamed. How to handle disgrace with grace is something Gladys never taught. I didn't push for it. The silence was golden. As long as I knew where he was and he knew where we were, in time, we'd all master the arts of civility, co-parenting and peace. I didn't want to deny Peter his daughter, but caring seemed to overwhelm him.

I hid between my empty pages; the notebooks that should have been filled with pithy details of my journey were not. Lupus' exhaustion had taken over and all that I had were snippets of thoughts that came over me like waves. I wrote with red ink only, scattering my words on snow-white pages, like blood. I often wrote to Peter, but my words were never intended for his eyes. It was a journal of "as ifs."

ENTRY:

I'm away from you. I like our current arrangement. I am free to reinvent myself. Thank you for this gift of hard lessons and the pain of what it means to love and to lose. Thank you for forcing me to rediscover myself and for dragging me through this mud bath.

Rain is almost three years old. She is thriving as best as she can with a mother who is healing and struggling every day to become whole. Rain has a few favorite words that she uses over and over again. "Up" (pick me up); "Ma-ma" (Mommy); "Ju-Ju" (juice); "Poo-poo" (I need to go to the bathroom); "Tee Tee" (TV); "Eeef" (Eat). She forgot "DaDa."

Dorian's mother, Estelle, had fallen in love with Rain. Since Dorian refused to settle down and give her a grandchild, Rain had become a stand-in. Estelle scooped her up in her arms and took her away during the days so she could love her in a motherly way and I could think about how I would live chronically ill, alone, and constantly needed by another.

I used to sit alone in Dorian's house realizing how long it had been since I felt joy. I had only been touched by Rain's tiny hands and sloppy kisses which were tainted by my persistent fear of catching something. I craved feelings other than fear, pain, and hatred. I wanted to feel the other parts of my body, the parts that are fed by music.

The buzzing of my cell phone indicated a text message from Dorian. It read: "Wanna come to a concert this weekend? Omar. My mom will watch Rain."

"Yes!" I texted with one hand. As soon as I pressed *Send*, I regretted it. I didn't want to leave Rain. I wasn't ready to go out, just yet. There is *no recourse in the electronic age.*

ENTRY:

Maybe it was my reckless creativity that made me think I wanted you. Maybe I thought you would be able to calm my Marigold chaos. Maybe I thought the suburbs would tame me. Maybe I was just a game for you: another girl that you snuck in without anyone seeing.

I glimpsed myself trying to look like Morgan, but everything had shifted in my face. Even the texture of my skin. There were signs of too much exposure to pain. I looked tired of trying to look like my old self.

Dorian came into the room as I got ready for the Omar show. The naked ceiling bulb in my borrowed bedroom dangled from the ceiling illuminating all of my flaws. There were no nuances or shadows, just the bluntness of my own homeliness. My eyes begged for a miracle. As he watched me get ready, Dorian was giddy. "Morgan, it'll be just like back-in-the-day. Remember all those free shows we used to go to?"

I had somehow forgotten the ecstasy of being with the music heads. I had forgotten how to lose myself.

"How do I look?" *Stupid question*. Dorian peered at my ragged locks and parched lips and said, "Better…Better than before."

"Thanks a lot!" My stomach sank. I wanted to cancel. Insecurity swept over me like a ghost.

"Just kidding. You look good. Let's go," he said.

As we approached Club Native, I felt dizzy. I had lost my grasp on how to be out at night, among seekers of fun. As we entered the club, the opening act was already on stage finishing her set. She was a large bronzed woman with a tight yellow turban pulling the skin around her eyes making her look exotic. Her face was pretty and drenched in perspiration as she belted out a soulful tune about yearning. It was a song that I didn't recognize, reminding me how much I had missed all those months without music. The audience was romanced by every note she sang. I closed my eyes and let the intensity of music grab me, shaking my fears away. The weed heads were staked out in the corners of the club smoking their way to a higher consciousness. The darkness in the room scared me slightly. *It had been so long.*

It was her last song, but the audience didn't want to release her. The crowd filled with dreadlocked bohemians stomped and shouted for more of the singer's deep dark voice. She reminded me of the new artists that I had worked with in the recording studio. They were always proud and mortified at the same time. She probably didn't have another song prepared. She was torn between bathing in her own glory for a few seconds longer and being embarrassingly unprepared. Her manager sharply signaled for her to leave the stage. "My record will be in stores in a couple of weeks. Look for me, y'all! Love y'all." And she was gone. The lights went up a little. The smoke draped around our shoulders like capes. The weed smokers burrowed further into their corners, not wanting to be too visible, yet wanting to be recognized for their powerful spiritual stench.

"Look at all the hotties in here. Look at that one with the bangin' ass." Dorian's head went from side to side. "Look at her – she has a really pretty face! Woohoo, I'm going to get on her." I was nauseated by the smoke and the sickness of not belonging. The more Dorian raved, the more I realized that I shouldn't be there. I was not one of those hotties. I would never be again. Eye contact and efforts to be noticed were no longer a part of my reality. I was desperate to be back in my borrowed room on my borrowed futon, with my daughter and my own private music.

Dorian said, "Excuse me while I go huntin'. Would you like a drink?"

"Water for me," I replied. "Don't forget the lemon." *Anti-oxidant.*

"You got it. I'll be back. Sit tight."

I found a pole that I could lean against. I was already feeling tired. The smoke was hurting my eyes and throat. *Sjogrens Syndrome is when the immune system attacks the glands that produce moisture in your body.* My throat and my eyes were desperate for moisture. Omar was about to grace the stage. The audience was getting restless like animals needing to be fed.

The multi-colored dreadlocked Omar appeared from out of the shadows – his signature spliff dangling from his lips. The jazzy funk boomed through the speakers. The girls were in awe while the men saluted him by blowing smoke at the stage. I was weak with embarrassment. *What was I doing here*? Omar spoke to the crowd with his British lilt, getting them wet with anticipation.

The first few bars signaled one of my favorites. As it boomed out of the speakers, I knew why I was there. I made myself comfortable against the pole, so I could give Omar my full attention. He opened the set with his inimitable scatting. His voice dug deep with every playful scat that he spat. His eyes were closed and his body was fluid with rhythm. He was sexy and free and reminded me of what I once desired; a man like that. *Someone comfortable in his own skin.*

Dorian returned from the bar with a pretty, young playmate. He had bought her a pink drink with a cherry on top. She had no idea that Dorian had already planned to sleep with her. He had already sealed his confidence by betting me $20 regarding the night's outcome, even before he had a face or a name. He would assure the playmate that I was his sister. Sometimes he said "cousin." This one was bone thin with pale translucent skin. Her teeth were white and she wore a tight red dress and blue contact lenses. Her nails were long and fake. I was so glad that Dorian and I never dated. For him women were just a game. I was comfortable that I was invisible to him, seen only as a "sister." The smoke was getting to me, clinging to my throat and burning my eyes.

Dorian was average height with a mane of curls that he grew just long enough to form a halo that framed his face. His eyes were dark and brooding. Dorian was a magnet for young pretty girls whose biggest aspiration was to be seen with someone who made them look good.

Dorian had forgotten my water. A *dry mouth means a compromised immune system.* He looked at me mouthing the words, "Your water. So sorry!"

Aloud he said, "Morgan, meet Miel. Her name means *honey* in Spanish. Isn't that fly?"

"Yes it is. Nice to meet you, Miel."

"You're Dorian's cousin, right?" she said with slight suspicion.

"Right."

Strengthened by my brother's thoughtlessness, I decided I could get my own water. As I started into the thick crowd, I said to the two of them, "I'll be back." I knew I could do what I was accustomed to doing; being on my own. I got a cup of lemon water from a bartender with a blue afro and a brow piercing. I noticed a door on the side of the bar that led to an outdoor patio. I grabbed my cup and dashed to get some fresh air. I sat on a bench staring at Atlanta's magnificent skyline, seeing what Marigold's birthplace had grown into, hoping that it would grow me, too.

I could feel eyes on me. I couldn't bear to look. "Excuse me, can I sit here?" I looked up frightened, not knowing what to do. I would be expected to be flirtatious; attractive; eager. I was none of the above, anymore.

"Yes...I mean, no. Of course. No problem," I stammered.

"Good. I noticed you across the room. How long have you been growing your locks?"

"A little less than a year," I said, reminded that my locks had been in my life for the same time as my Lupus.

I dared to look at him. He surprised me. His voice was slow and warm like syrup; the sound of a black man – but he was Japanese. His hair was straight and long and poured down his back like black coffee. I was taken aback by his perfect chiseled face.

"Are you enjoying the show?" he said into my ear, as I looked straight ahead at the buildings, frightened by eye contact, hoping I would not stare.

"Yeah. I love Omar. But the smoke's getting to me." I sounded like a senior citizen.

"Me too!" he said. "I can't stand smoke. It's strange being that I'm a DJ and I'm used to it. When I'm not in the booth, it seems worse."

"You're a DJ?" When I finally dared to look in his face, he was not only a DJ, his face was irresistible. He had long eyelashes and silver hoops in both ears. His jeans were torn, just loose enough and black. His sleeveless T-shirt was fitted, showcasing his muscular frame. Celtic tattoos shrouded his arms. I couldn't help but stare and imagine his arms all over me.

"Yeah. I'm new to Atlanta and just started spinning a few months ago. I worked a lot in New York, where I'm from."

"Me too," I said.

"Are you a DJ? Or are you from New York?"

"From New York. And I *wish* I were a DJ," I clarified.

"You do? Why wish when you could do it?"

"Being a DJ is a fantasy. Feeding a hungry crowd with music and all of that but…"

"Spinning is real cool…What's your name?"

"Morgan. What's yours?"

"Kweku. Maybe I can teach you to spin sometime."

"That's a dreamy offer, but I can't take you up on it."

"Why not?"

"We're not really settled yet, so I can't commit to anything. We're staying with a friend. We just moved here, too."

"Who's we?"

"Me and my daughter."

"What kind of a friend are you staying with? A boyfriend?" Kweku asked.

"No. A real friend. He's like my brother." *A careless brother*.

"Do you think I could get your number?" He asked.

What was Kweku doing? What did he want from me? I wasn't a regular girl; no longer a hottie. I will take medicine for the rest of my life. I am no longer spontaneous. I can't have sex because I take immune-suppressing drugs. I am doomed to a life of moderation. If he knew these things about me, he wouldn't want my number.

I tried to get out of it, but Kweku was staring at me with insistence. I stumbled, "I have an Arizona cell phone number." *The dumbest thing I could have said.*

"And?" he said.

I took a deep breath and I exhaled the digits, "520-471-3355." Kweku punched the numbers into his silver cell phone. *The last time I gave my phone number to a man, it was Peter.*

"Cool. I'll give you a call. Maybe we can go dancing sometime. I bet you're a good dancer."

A smile spread across my face and Kweku saw it. "I'll call you soon. I should get goin'. I'm workin' tonight at an afterhours spot in Midtown. "

"Have a good night," I said.

"You too, talk to you soon." Kweku sauntered across the patio and back into the club. Smoke clouds made it impossible for me to admire his tall silhouette one last time.

Omar was taking a break from his set. The lights had gone up again and smoke formed a cloud over the crowd. The house DJ had put on some dance music and I wished I was unencumbered enough to dance alone, like I used to.

Dorian and Kweku passed each other as Kweku went back into the club and Dorian came to see where I had gone.

"Where did Miel go?" I asked him.

"She's waiting for me inside, but I've been looking everywhere for you. I saw you doin' your thang with that guy. The old Morgan is finally back and she's in the ATL! How'd you like the show? Omar is amazing isn't he?"

The old Morgan is dead.

"Yeah it's great from what I can hear out here. There's too much smoke inside. I had to come outside to breathe."

"Morgan, you sound like an old lady. Lighten up. You'll get used to it. Live a little."

ENTRY:

Loving is inconvenient. It makes one sweat too much and too often. It made me become who I wasn't. We both spent too much of our lives trying to be what we thought we should.

Kweku called.

Frightened.

Dorian's mother, Estelle, had been so excited that I was getting out of the house; she jumped at the chance to keep Rain again. She said a real date would be good for me. She too worried that I was depressed. "Every young woman should have male company," she said. "You go out and have a great time. Rain will be my Saturday night date." Dorian's father was also a Mason so he was never home. He was always at lodge meetings wearing a funny hat and speaking in code.

I knew this night with Kweku would have no time for illness, severe fatigue, or curfews. Dorian was out of town and I had the whole house to myself to fuss and fret about Kweku. I stood in front of the mirror much longer than I had in what seemed like a decade, trying to get my hair to look effortlessly tossed and groomed at the same time. I had scrubbed my face and applied as much mascara as my thin lashes could hold. My eyebrows had faded recently without my knowledge. *Hair loss can occur.* I had bought a black brow pencil to darken them. I hadn't ever attempted to fill them in. My hand shook. My lines were uneven.

ENTRY:

If we try too hard, we lose sight and no one knows what they are looking at.

When the doorbell rang, I nearly tripped and fell over one of Rain's toys. I smoothed myself out and walked to the door, my ankle smarted and threatened to swell. Kweku rang the doorbell again. I opened the door and Kweku was sexy and strange and attractive all at once. I felt warm all over my body. He looked at me and said, "Hey, lady, you look good. I brought you something." Instantly, I recognized his dramatic tattoos. I wanted to touch them.

He reached into his messenger bag and pulled out eight CDs, five mixed discs and three that were albums that he produced. I felt like someone had just given me the sun and the moon.

"Thank you. I wasn't expecting this. These are all yours?"

Kweku said proudly, "Yeah, pretty much. I produced all of them and some of the albums are just remixes – but it is mostly house music, cause I know you like it."

"I do. Thank you." *What will he want from me?*

"I'm almost ready," I said, needing to look at my unruly hair one more time.

I went back to my room and looked in the mirror. Nothing had changed. I was nervous about what this night would hold for me and my disease. Which would prevail in the face of music's grip? Lupus or Life?

Kweku held the door of his car for me. He was a gentleman. He was part of a DJ Collective of mostly Japanese DJs that I read about in a magazine. I wanted to ask him about it, but I realized it would be cooler to act like I already knew everything I needed to know about them and him. The CDs all bore a logo which looked a lot like Kweku's tattoos. I figured I would look up their meaning later. Kweku looked young. His skin was supple and clear. His eyes sparkled with music.

"So, how did you end up in Atlanta?" he asked as he started the car. One of his house CDs came on with the engine.

"Long story. My mother was born here. And I'm getting a divorce."

"Oh. I just got mine finalized."

"Really? I'm sorry to hear that."

"Yes. I was married for four years. I was 22. Then my wife fell in love with a woman," he said with ease.

"How do you feel about that?"

"It's cool. I actually understand. Different strokes. She and I are still good friends. Her girlfriend is really good for her. My ex-wife needed a woman. A man could never make her happy."

Listening to Kweku talk, I started to relax. *I wanted to understand more about his ex-wife and why Kweku couldn't please her. I didn't want to pry. He had moved on.* "You have a child?" I heard him say.

"Yes. Rain is her name."

"Great name."

I didn't know what else I wanted to share with him. I had shared already more than I was ready to.

The hard rain took our attention. Kweku concentrated on the wet dark road and I worried that he was not a good enough driver to get us there without incident. *What would happen to Rain if I were in an accident?*

He said, "We need the rain. It was a drought last week."

"I don't think you know what a drought looks like. I lived in Arizona."

When we got to The Lounge, it was raining too hard to get out of the car. He turned to face me and said, "Let's just park, while the rain subsides."

"I don't know anything about parking," I said weakly. I shuddered at my awkwardness.

Kweku ignored my hesitancy. He didn't care about my pitiful attempts to divert his flirtation. He boldly grabbed a non-sequitur. "So, what was the wildest thing that you have ever done?"

He was talking about sex. I didn't have anything to share. I considered making something up, but I didn't really have a reservoir from which to draw. I had been married to Peter for nearly nine years. We had spent our time growing apart and not together. All of my wildness had dried up.

Kweku listened as I mumbled excuses and ignoring me, he leaned over and planted the sweetest kiss on my left cheek. His kiss felt soft and innocent and tender like rose petals. What did he see that was left of me? "I love your smile. I just really have a need to kiss you. Do you mind?"

Lupus came to center stage.

I said looking toward the club, "I can't. It's a long story. I'll tell you about it later. Let's go inside and dance."

Kweku responded, "Can't wait to hear this one. I still want my real kiss, lady."

"Later. I promise. We have a long night ahead of us. Let's pace ourselves," I said, sounding schoolmarmish.

I had several hours to second guess the doctors. What will happen if I kiss the wrong lips? Will their simple cold turn into pneumonia? Would mere exposure to a venereal disease give it to me full-blown? Could kissing give me AIDS? What did Dr. Valdez call it?...opportunistic infections. How can I avoid them? I was reaching for Morgan and feeling her slip out of my fingers. What lesson was God forcing me to learn? He had heard my cries. How could He have started to restore my body and not let me drink from the nectar of my own essence?

The Lounge was a club under the freeway. The doorway was narrow and opened into a wide entrance that made you feel as though you were going into a dungeon. The rancid smoke greeted us as Kweku paid the bouncer, who stood just outside the door. By the time we got down the ramp our clothes already reeked of late night debauchery.

A familiar song jumped from the nine-foot speakers that lined the walls of the club. The house music was like an infrared zone into which you could walk and take a load off. Faces blurred through the dark smoke. I was with my people again. The people who love music like Christians love Jesus. Everyone was loose and slippery with sweat. We all shared a collective obedience to the beat. Our bodies did what the beats told us to do.

"Would you like a drink?" Kweku asked, his head already bobbing. The music bore down on us like hail. Our teeth glowed spookily from the florescent black lights.

"Water would be good," I shouted over the beats. "With lemon."

Standing still under the music made me nervous. I tapped my foot and bobbed my head. Out of the corner of my wandering eye, I saw someone approaching me. "Wanna dance," he yelled? I was just about to say yes when Kweku walked toward me with a beer in one hand and a cup of lemon water in the other. I smiled politely and moved toward Kweku. I had not really danced in years, maybe at weddings with Peter, but not like this. Not with a room full of real music heads. Kweku put the bottle and cup down on a shelf. He moved into me and my arms stretched out for him to fit in a little closer to my body.

I started moving slowly. The music started to blur my eyes making it easier for me to crawl inside of myself. My eyes slowly fell shut. I felt my hips start to sway in a way that I only faintly remembered from the throes of passion. It was a relentless sway. My hips were on a swivel operated by spirit. I was being entered by some unknown force that was irresistible, luscious, and dripping with *bliss.*

Young men and women surrounded us. I mistook them for distant faces from my New York past. *It couldn't be them, because time had passed.* Music heads all look the same. We had all been raised in smoky musty rooms with a DJ giving us the food that we needed from a booth. We had all been baptized like this.

A man to my left was yelling and speaking in tongues, jumping and screaming as though something was coming after him. *Music.* His calls mimicked those coming from the speakers. He was exhilarated as if in a sacred ceremony. He was flapping his arms like a wild loon coming out of the water. He seemed to be flying over the dance floor, his sweat showering us all with our religion.

Kweku placed his warm hand underneath my shirt and I shuddered, feeling the electricity that arises with touch. I yearned to touch him, too, but tripped on a new fixation with earthly concerns. Kweku danced slowly, trying to catch my hips. I didn't know what they were doing, but I just knew that they were making everything wet inside and out. I felt Kweku's hands on my bare skin, gliding up and down my back. He whispered into my ear, "Is this okay?"

When I was in this place, everything was okay. Music takes me to a sacred place.

I was trapped between wishing and needing; a fork in the road. I had to choose.

CHAPTER 14 | *Choices*

Atlanta, Georgia, 2005

I made a choice. Kweku grabbed me around my waist and kissed me in the parking lot of R. Thomas, a 24-hour vegetarian restaurant. I fell right into his kiss. My tongue was ravenous for the indescribable taste of affection. I kissed Kweku for what seemed like an hour in the deserted parking lot; restaurant staff staring at us with envy. I worried *not* about repercussions.

As he drove me home we didn't speak; we were both speechless, feverish with insatiability. As soon as we were parked, we kissed again, exhaustingly, while the night wrapped us in anonymity. I was so tired that my knees buckled underneath me, but I couldn't get enough of being connected.

He wanted to stay with me, but I discouraged him, explaining that I had to pick Rain up in the morning from Estelle's. All of the real reasons went unsaid. Peter had slowly seeped out of my mind like fuzzy memories of kindergarten. Only the rest of my life with Rain filled my head. I regretted and accepted that I would never see Kweku again. There would be no room.

I set the alarm giving myself only four precious hours before I would be forced to wake up with intention and responsibility. When I rolled over the next morning, I checked my cell phone for messages. There were two; Roy with his daily check-in and surprisingly, Allegra from Eastside Girls Academy, calling from London. She left a message that she needed to talk to me.

I decided not to call either one of them then and retrieve Rain, whom I suddenly missed with urgency. I dressed hurriedly, washed my face, applied mascara and lip gloss, and fluffed my locks and put a red bandana around them to keep them out of my face. I pulled one of Kweku's CDs off the dining room table, where I left them in a hurry the night before. The drive downtown filled me up with peace and anxiety. *I really was on my own. I was all that Rain had.* Kweku's House music CD filled me with visions of the night before; dancing and losing myself.

Although Estelle was enthusiastic about my date, as I drove towards her, I feared that she would ask me for details. She would want to know if Kweku came from a good family. She would want to know if he was *marriage material.* She would ask me *where* he took me to dinner. She would ask me *how I felt* about him. I didn't have any of the answers that she wanted. She wouldn't want to know that I kissed him without any *need* for a future. As I drove bobbing my head to Kweku's mixes I hoped that Rain hadn't broken anything in Estelle's fancy house. Rain was just starting to touch everything in sight, and if she wasn't touching it, she was knocking it over.

When I arrived at Estelle's, she and Rain were sitting on the front porch. She was playing with a little green ball that had recently held her in rapture. When she saw me, her face widened and Estelle pulled her closer while she pulled away trying to get to me.

"Hi baby! How are you?" I walked over to them relieved that she was still as happy and as healthy as I left her. I planted a kiss on Rain's cheek.

She responded, "Ma Ma, Ma Ma," reaching out for me.

"Hello, Dear," Estelle said as I approached. "Did you have a good time last evening?"

"Excellent. Thank you again for keeping Rain. Two Saturday nights in a month! You're an angel."

"You deserve it, honey."

"How was Rain?" I asked with trepidation.

"She was great. I'll look forward to taking her next week too, if that's OK with you? I love this time in their little lives. Rain reminds me of when Dorian was that age. I so miss the feeling of being needed." Estelle reminisced, her wide smile reminded me of Dorian's.

That was the thing that terrified me the most about mothering. She needed me for everything while I needed *me* more. I had taken her out of Estelle's arms and her tiny fingers were immediately tangled in my hair. "Stop," I whispered to her, trying to keep my gaze on Estelle's cloudy eyes. The more I whispered "stop," to her, the more she heard "do it more."

Estelle continued, "Dorian barely calls me anymore. He's always on the road with those hooligans in that rock group. Dorian gets irritated when I tell him that I miss him. My husband says that I'm a whiner. I can't seem to get it right with my two men. But when I'm with Rain, I feel like I'm doing what's needed and at least *she* appreciates it. Don't you, Baby?" Estelle turned to Rain, smashing her own nose against hers.

"*I* appreciate it more than you know. I'm feeling better and finally getting my bearings around Atlanta. I'll have her ready whichever day you want her. Thank you. This time you're giving me is a gift."

"I have all kinds of plans for us," Estelle said excitedly. "I'm going to take her to the park and to the zoo, if we have time. Please pack some extra supplies this time. She needs to be changed more often than you think. Perhaps, Morgan, once you get settled, you may consider taking some parenting classes. It couldn't hurt."

Estelle, Estelle, Estelle. Dorian said you were rude. Stuttering and staring at the gap in her front teeth, I finally got my mouth to say, "No, it couldn't hurt. Thank you for everything. Rain let's go." I hurried, worried that Estelle would talk more and I just wanted to get back into the car and listen to the sounds of Kweku.

When I got back to Dorian's house there was an email from Allegra.

Morgan,

I've tried to reach you by phone. Please email me when are you available. I will call then.

Allegra

Five years before, Peter and I had gone to Paris for Allegra and Newlen's wedding. After high school, Allegra had attended Paris-Sorbonne University, got a masters degree in International politics and stayed in Paris. The reason she stayed shocked us. It wasn't shocking that she met a man. It was not shocking that she would eventually marry him. What was shocking was that he was not a *white* man. He was a black man. Newlen was the son of a diplomat. Allegra never mentioned it until we all saw him at their wedding. They moved to London for his commercial real estate business. *EGA girls were so full of surprises.*

When Allegra heard about my illness through the EGA grapevine, she emailed me immediately and we fell right back into the friendship that we had started so many years before in high school dance club.

Their wedding said it all. Allegra got her dream; she married an older wealthy man. They already had twin boys, Hugh and Harvey, and one on the way. Allegra had always been a nurturer despite her super-intelligent mind. She worked as a researcher from home for a company based in Kansas. I still think about the night of Marigold's death when she held my hand through the night.

When Allegra shared with Newlen that I was sick and that Peter and I were divorcing, she got the green light to be generous, EGA-style. I suspected that Allegra was calling to tell me that she wanted to send money. Giving money to those less fortunate was their private philanthropy. Roy never trusted it. "Never take money from friends. It's the fastest way to lose them."

I emailed her:

Allegra -

I'm home.

The phone rang almost instantaneously.

"Hello?"

"Morgan?" she said.

I was proud to say, "Glad you caught me, I've been out all weekend."

"Newlen and I have talked and we want to fly you over to London."

"Allegra, why would you do that for me?"

"February 9, 1981. Since that day, I've always wanted to do something to show you how much I cared. When your mother died something in me shattered. Losing a mother is unthinkable. Now, I finally can show you how sorry I was when I had nothing to say or to give you. All I could do was hold your hand."

"And I will never forget that." I was stunned that after all these years, Allegra remembered the day of Marigold's death. "I still don't know what to say to an invitation like that."

"Just say, yes," she said.

"Yes. When? What about Rain?" My head swirled with memories of London and the semester that brought me back to life after Marigold died. I felt short of breath, afraid to say anything in case I was dreaming too hard.

Allegra broke in, "Will you bring Rain? – Hugh and Harvey would be thrilled to have a little girl to play with."

I didn't hesitate. "I don't think so. I feel like I may be coming alive again. I need time to get ready for everything that awaits us. I need to be alone. You understand…"

"What *will* you do with Rain? Have you heard from Peter?" Allegra asked.

"Haven't heard from him in several months. We're out of things to say. He'll surface again some time. We both have a lot to work out for ourselves. I think I know the perfect someone who would love to keep Rain. I'll check with her and get back to you." I was embarrassed but had to say to Allegra, "The other problem is that I'm completely broke. My father is helping me out and because you know him, you know it's not a friendly loan. I may not even be able to swing this at all. Rain and I don't even have an address. We're staying with my friend, Dorian, until I know what to do next."

"Newlen and I will take care of everything."

"Are you sure that's OK with him? I feel funny—"

"Funny why? You're one of my oldest friends. EGA girls are sisters for life. It's Newlen's duty to help me help my sister. That's just how it works in this house. Just let me know a couple of possible dates and we will get this done. Start planning for a much-needed break from all this terrible stuff that you've been going through."

"I will."

Allegra replied, "I love you, Morgan and I can't wait to lay eyes on you. Just remember, shit doesn't last forever. I'll email you. Au revoir!"

"Shit" sounded so foreign coming out of Allegra's proper mouth. That's why I loved her. After all that time, she was still that awkward girl from the Lower East Side who rode the subway downtown to the village when the village was considered just as bad as Harlem. Despite her new life, she could still recognize "shit" when she saw it.

Guilt tackled me. I felt guilty planning a trip without Rain, but I knew that some time in London could return me to myself. Estelle was thrilled that she would have uninterrupted time with Rain. With her, Rain would be cared for and spoiled while I found the lost pieces of my puzzle. I consoled myself; *Rain will never remember these bumpy years.*

I was eager to tell Roy. It was important that he knew that good deeds by people with white skin were possible. 400 years had damaged him, mangling his perspective of all people white and rich. Roy always likened them to "devils."

Roy sighed as I explained the details and logistics of the invitation and then he said with exasperation, "Why would Allegra do that? What's her ulterior motive?"

"Daddy, maybe she just loves me and wants to see me get some relief from the 'shit,' as she called it."

Roy said, softening, "Those girls did love you. I hate to admit it. They've been with you through it all."

"Don't hate to admit it. Just admit it," I said.

"What are you gonna do with Rain? I'll keep her. When you leaving?"

"You'd keep her?"

"I have no choice. But, Ava, there you go running again. You just can't stay put. You ran to Arizona to get away from New York, you ran to Atlanta to get away from Arizona. I don't know what you're doing and I don't want to pay for anymore of these bright ideas that you have. You're a mother now. You have to think differently. It's not all about you, anymore. You're just like ya Mama."

Stung. "I have to get off the phone now," I said, shrinking.

"Don't throw me off – you just don't want to hear what I'm saying," Roy said.

He was right. I was a runner. Just like Marigold. She and I had both been "over exposed" and left with unrealistic images fogging up our brains. When things didn't turn out we ran. She ran to death. I was desperate to find myself amongst the ruins. Then I could be strong again. Healthy again. Ready to be Rain's mother. But not until then.

After too many moments of silence, I said, "If it's not all about me, how can I be about Rain?" I felt tears building inside my eyes. *Daddy always does this to me. He always turns the screw deeper.* "I have to go, Daddy, really. I have to be somewhere."

"Where'd *you* have to be?" he said with ire.

I put the phone back into its cradle, disconnecting without ceremony. Then, I said, aloud, "London."

The very next morning this email came from Allegra…

Morgan-

I'm thinking about 2 ½ weeks. Have you looked at dates? You know Newlen and I live in Stratford, about two and a half hours outside of London. I was thinking that it may be quite nice for you to spend some time alone in the country. I know you have a close friend in London. What was her name again? Marta? Perhaps we can even coordinate it so that we are on holiday for most of it so you can have some privacy. Tell me so I can book…
– Allegra

I first found the missing pieces of myself in London after Marigold's death. I had been a drooping flower from the 8th grade until junior year of college when London brought me to life. When I closed my eyes I could still see the lights surrounding Trafalgar Square after the clubs let out. I could still smell the packed late night fish and chip shops that peppered the square. I could still hear the rowdy night bus crowds, cursing politely with greasy French Fries spilling out of over-stuffed mouths. And most of all I remembered *Magda*. An important part of me had been left there with her.

The three weeks before my trip Peter was still not calling. Gladys had stopped calling too, save for one apologetic voice message saying that Peter had instructed her not to call me. She said that she missed us. She also said that she felt obligated to honor her Peacock. She promised to send money if I promised that Peter would never know.

London, England May, 2005

I arrived at Heathrow airport at the crack of London's dawn. It had been fifteen years after my semester abroad and five since Peter and I transferred in London, heading for Allegra and Newlen's wedding in Paris. Heathrow Airport looked the same, only smokier. I nearly felt the same, only humbled. My carry-on was bulging with Cellcept, Plaquenil, Predisone, vitamins, masks, ointments, and a book of symptoms and what to do if a flare strikes unexpectedly. The bag was bulging with things that inhibit freedom, making me feel as though my boots were stuck in cement.

I was immediately struck by the buzz of people; the smoke, the malodorous smell of cheap coffee and breakfasty smells of pastries and sugar. I could see and hear pretty boys all around me with British accents talking on their cell phones. I wished I had the energy to flirt.

I walked down the endless and trashy corridor through the airport to get to the Tube station where I would catch the train to Paddington Station. From Paddington Station I would then travel to Stratford-Upon-Avon. *Leave it to Allegra to live in Shakespeare's birthplace. That's so Eastside Girls Academy.* My body awkwardly struggled with a too-heavy garment bag on one side and my carry-on on the other. My legs begged me to stop for rest. I resisted. Trickles of perspiration beaded my forehead. I felt hot under my skin. *Lupus' low grade fever.* When I reached the confusing ticket kiosks that lined the foyer, I got a ticket and cursed how poorly I had packed. I had forgotten how much had changed in me, while nothing seemed to have changed around me.

After the two hour ride from Heathrow to Paddington Station, I finally arrived at Track 1 for my 12:30 train to Stratford-Upon-Avon, where Allegra and Newlen had purchased an eight bedroom house on 15 acres soon after their wedding.

I arrived at the dingy Stratford train station and Newlen Tanning was waiting for me. His mocha skin had aged and his curly hair was grayer than at the wedding, but he still was the distinguished gentleman of Allegra's dreams. Newlen saw me looking for Allegra.

"She's at home with the boys," he said coming up behind me. "They are coming down with something, and she didn't want to go too far away from them." Newlen smiled at me, gave me a warm embrace, grabbed my bag off my shoulder and started talking as if I had been in conversation with him all morning. "She's extremely anxious to see you. She has prepared a great lunch. Hope you're hungry. By the way, you look well, Morgan, especially after what you've been through. I don't want to overstep my boundaries, but I am very sorry that you are going through a divorce and an illness." He headed toward the small navy blue Mercedes that was parked illegally right at the front of the station. Newlen had gained weight and looked happy. He was sixteen years our senior, wealthy and had landed himself a younger smart woman of childbearing years.

He gave me an abridged but formal tour as we drove through the historic town of Stratford-Upon-Avon. "There are some brilliant shops downtown. Did you see the shop with Shakespearean clothes?"

"Yes. I saw it," I said struggling for enthusiasm. *On my budget, I was just glad to be there with no plans of going into town.* Newlen couldn't seem to fathom the bitter taste of not-having and so he spoke as if it was a given that I would go shopping and touring around. *He must have forgotten that he had paid for me to be there.*

My mind drifted as the car dug deeper into the English countryside. The manicured valleys sprinkled with sheep and cows made for a magnificent postcard. The dips in the terrain were surreal. I was no longer listening to Newlen as he droned on about the lagging commercial real estate market in London. I was lost in the corridor of my own imagination.

We arrived at the house which was stone gray. The house was made of boulders with oversized black shutters that highlighted the abundance of rooms inside. Allegra greeted me at the side of the house with Hugh and Harvey under her heels. Allegra was still striking with dark shiny hair, hazel eyes, and a swarthy complexion. Allegra Rocklidge Tanning was not a WASP, but the WASPs claimed her as their own. Allegra always carried herself as though she was born to be royalty, even though she and her younger sister grew up with a single parent in a one-bedroom apartment on the border of Chinatown. Her petite body exposed the impending birth of her third child. Allegra's stocky nanny, Stacy, barreled out of the side door sweeping Hugh and Harvey out of the way so she could greet me in peace. I could only glimpse their little feet, beige complexions, and jet black curls as Stacy shooed them past me like fireflies.

Hugging Allegra was like hugging all the years that hung between us. The first thing Allegra did after asking Newlen to take my bags up to my room was launch me onto a tour of their grounds. *Exhausted and desperate to sit.*

"Morgan, let's go this way. This is the prettier view…"

Allegra was wearing oversized brown sunglasses with the logo of the designer emblazoned on both sides, impossible to miss. She wore the most expensive gardening gear that included high boots for walking through tall grass and water. Emblazoned on the boots was a small but prominent rubber seal that simply read "W." I was proud to be standing in the midst of Allegra's dreams.

The jet lag was making me wobble. I was slightly dizzy and my ears were ringing. I wished to lie down on the grass to nap, but she insisted on talking and touring. I caught her odd new accent that she had acquired as a European. It was a mix of British English, French, and New York City.

"Would you like a cup of tea?" she asked. I imagined a small bell in her pocket that she would ring and Stacy would come running out to serve us. But since I declined, she didn't have to ring it.

I was struck by the irony of Allegra and I standing in her good life. *Such different lives but together again to save a life, if just for a moment.*

Once inside the house, Allegra talked more and faster. She showed me room after room; light switches and temperature control panels; bathrooms and bookshelves. Linen closets, towels, how to use the washing machine. I couldn't hold it all in my head. I was too sleepy. I was eager to be left alone to hide between my pages hoping to emerge with answers. I prayed that soon Allegra would leave me alone to wander, dream, and imagine what my life would be after this ordeal.

Allegra glided above the carpet pointing, grimacing, and apologizing for the slightest imperfections of her perfect home. When we ascended the grand staircase, the upper level of the house was just as pristine from all views, except for the negligible evidence of lucky little boys living there. I noticed a stray brown crayon that Stacy must have missed and a deflated balloon shriveled and dead.

When we reached the landing, Allegra directed us towards the guest room and said, "Here's your room, Morgan. Your bathroom is just through there..." She pointed a long finger towards a small hallway to the side of my room that led down two steps into an airy bathroom with a skylight that seemed to be glowing with sunlight. *I would care about it later.*

Allegra continued with her tour, "In the morning, Stacy comes and will make breakfast for you, if you like. You're on your own for lunch as I told her that you needed to be left alone. The fridge is jammed with lots of good stuff."

My bedroom was bright and reminded me of the overly floral bedrooms of our childhood friends with the country houses and immigrant maids. Allegra's decor was Laura Ashley but tasteful; blues, not pink. The curtains and the carpet were both cornflower blue, the walls stark white. The furniture was antique blonde wood and the ornate antique canopy bed was dressed with a white sheer curtain.

"Morgan, now that we are alone for a minute, tell me how you really are. You are keeping up a strong front, but I don't buy it for a second. You must be heartbroken. How could Peter do this to his family?"

Allegra's touch was familiar. She caressed my hand in the same way that she did in 1981. She took my hand and walked me over to sit on the downy bed. We both sat. I feared that I would snore.

"I'm OK, really Allegra. Like I told you, Peter doesn't call us right now. But I know that will change. We both need time. Peter just couldn't handle it all. Believe it or not, I'm not as bitter as I was. Now, I'm just numb. I take responsibility for the things that I did, too."

"Morgan, there's no excuse! Why are you making one?" Allegra said with her brow furrowed, "A decent man would never abandon his child like Peter has. What did you do wrong except give that nobody the opportunity to claim *you* as his wife?"

I never knew that Allegra considered Peter "a nobody." I was in no position to defend him anymore. "Lots of things," I said. "Too much to tell. Just when you think you commit some negligible offense, you never knew what would 'do it all in' until it's all done."

"Morgan, what could you have done that was so bad?" Allegra persisted.

"Nothing that I intended to do. I just did what felt right at the time and it turns out it wasn't right…for him."

"'Right' according to whom? So, you leave Peter blameless in all of this?"

"Not at all. He has a lifetime to figure it out. This past year has been a river flowing underneath us. I don't want to drown. I have to stay afloat to get Rain to safety." I took a liberty and kicked off my tight shoes. *My ankles were throbbing, swollen and spilling out of the sides of my shoes. Edema.* They made a loud sound as they hit the polished hardwood floor.

I fell back on the pillow and diverted the attention from myself to her. I was tired of talking. "Allegra, how are *you*?"

She sat up straighter, "I am just how you see me. Big house. Big life. Enough money. Empty bed. The twins are lovely, but this life is depressing me."

"And you have one more on the way?" I asked barely able to keep my eyes open.

"I felt I was doing the right thing. I was doing what EGA girls are taught to do: go for the good life. Trade in soul for solitude. Newlen's never home. Newlen wanted lots of children. He grew up an only child. Why didn't anyone tell us that there was a chance that we could no longer want what we thought we wanted?"

"What is it that you wanted?" I asked, my eyes closing.

"I don't know, I guess. I never had time to figure it out. I was busy doing what seemed to make everyone around me happy and proud."

"Eastside Girls Academy made us all want things we didn't know were possible until we witnessed our peers having them, leaving us only to want. At least that's what it did to me. That Eastside mentality drove Marigold to drink and it made me sick. I traveled the path that she set out for me; private school, a college degree, a marriage, a career, and then my body stopped it all. It obviously wasn't my path."

"I couldn't believe when I heard that you were sick. You have been through enough, losing your mother at 15. How could all of this have happened to you?"

"Why not me? Something *happens* to everyone. *This* is what happened to you," I said eyeing her splendor.

"What happens if I don't want it anymore?" Allegra said, eyes watering.

"You'll leave corpses, just like I had to," I said as my eyes were shutting. I could feel her familiar caress as I fell into sleep's arms.

Allegra turned off the light as she left me to sleep through my first day in London.

CHAPTER 15 | *Peace and Quiet*

Stratford-Upon-Avon, England May, 2005

I woke up alone with silence all around. Dusk was starting to fall outside of the guest room window. I rose, as if from the dead, to find a note:

Sorry for talking your ear off this afternoon. So glad you're here. We've gone to Paris for a week. Enjoy your stay. Will call you with your London hotel information. I meant to tell you all of this but you fell asleep.

Lunch is in the kitchen. Enjoy.

-A

I sat back down on the side of the bed, afraid to touch any of Allegra's pristine things. I had fallen asleep on top of the blanket and Allegra had left me that way. The throw pillow that held my head was glaringly white and I feared that my hair would leave a stain. I peeked. It was only a small grey smudge of gel. *Dammit.*

I was disoriented. Struggling to believe that I was actually in England, a place that I thought I would never see again. It was 6:38 pm. I had slept through the lunch that Allegra made for me. I was starving. My stomach growled. I needed to call Estelle to check on Rain. I had only glimpsed Hugh and Harvey before Stacy whisked them away. I had never been fond of children until Rain. She had changed me, perhaps the way that I had changed Marigold. *Children force us to realize that it's not all about us.* I was twisted with yearning for the sweetness of Rain's smell while glad to be away from the weight of her existence. It was 1:38 p.m. in America, in Georgia, at Estelle's house; where she had my precious daughter to whom she was giving the motherly love that had been drained from my body. Allegra had said that I could use her phone anytime.

I fumbled with the compact cordless phone, punching in too many numbers, getting the codes all wrong. Too many zeros and in all the wrong places. Finally, a British operator came on and gave me irritated instructions on how to reach America, specifically Georgia, the city of Atlanta, the corner that housed Estelle and my Rain.

When I followed the instructions, the beeps and tones finally ceased and a long familiar American ring rang into my ear. I was relieved briefly until it just rang and rang, until a machine with Estelle's voice answered:

You have reached the Broadnax family. Please leave your name and number and we will return your call as soon as possible. Thank you. Have a pleasant day.

It hurt that there was no acknowledgment of their little house guest, Rain Holmes, the little motherless girl. I left an awkward message:

Raindrop, this is your mama....I miss you, baby. I'll see you soon. I promise. Estelle – thanks for doing this. I have arrived safely. I'll call again soon. I promise.

As I put the phone back into the cradle, I could feel my eyes moist with guilt's dew. If Rain had been with me, I would have been out of sorts, caught between the past, the present and the daunting future. *This time with Estelle is good for her, too. She is a mother when I can't be.* I opened the door and peered out into the spacious hallway. The grand staircase summoned me down.

I had already been in Allegra's kitchen on the tour, but I was re-impressed with how large and spare it was. A white porcelain plate covered in plastic awaited me. It sat at the other end of a long countertop. The only other things on the counter were three oversized glass canisters brimming with oats, brown rice and pound coins as if they were only pennies. I could see under the clear wrap what Allegra had prepared: sliced strawberries, smoked salmon, pita chips, raw broccoli, and carrots. I was ravenous. After looking around to make sure I was alone, I tore the plastic off furiously. As I filled my mouth with broccoli florets, I went to Allegra's mammoth refrigerator looking for something to dip the stalks into. Among the plethora of bottles, cans, jars and containers were many dressings. A yellow sauce intrigued me and it was the nearest. I reached into the cold refrigerator and pulled out the bottle, took off the cap and poured the dressing over the vegetables, drowning them. The sauce was similar to honey mustard but tangier. I disregarded the mess I was making. I dipped a carrot into the dressing and it clung stubbornly to my finger tips. Without swallowing the carrot completely, I stuffed a thick piece of the smoked salmon into my mouth to mingle with the carrot. *Salty and sweet*. The golden dressing oozed out of my mouth. I sopped up the excess with a wagging tongue. I chuckled to myself over the sight I must have been. The sound of my chewing echoed.

With my lips doused in yellow, I peered outside the kitchen into an expansive dining room – it was more like a banquet hall, easily seating 16 or 20. Beyond that room was another room, a sitting room decorated with leather couches and angled low tables. I left the mess on the counter to see it all. I cautiously peered at all of the things that comprised Allegra's new life. I touched the framed pictures from the beach, admired the size of the leather-bound *Great Expectations*. I frowned at the abstract textured oil paintings and the baroque antiques. I laughed inside knowing that Allegra could not have picked these things. Allegra had been sucked in to the quicksand. *She had arrived. Her house was like the houses of the rich girls that we grew up with.* My head started to ache, trying to forget my own drowned accoutrements.

I started to feel uncomfortable probing, assessing, and regretting. I went back up to my room to unpack my things and put something down on empty pages.

Looking for a pen, I flicked the pages of my A-Z London travel guide. There was no pen, just a letter from Magda that fell out of the center.

The last time Magda and I had spoken had been a month before my wedding. She had warned me not to do it. She reminded me of all of the promises we had made to each other: to remain free and independent. She reminded me that we promised to be bold. That was the last time we spoke. There was no love lost between us. It had just been a difference of opinion. She wouldn't have understood all that I had been through with Roy and without Marigold. She wouldn't have understood the choices that I had to make.

Magda's email address had stayed the same after all those years. I had written her to tell her that I was coming to London. I had emailed little else. She responded the way I thought she would:

...Really? I'm all bundled up inside thinking of your arrival. I will try to hold on to my rushing thoughts. I am breathless with excitement. Counting the minutes.

Always,

Magdalene

I hadn't known what to expect from a girl wearing a turban on her head when she approached me at Club Heaven in London in 1986. "You `ave a light?" Magda had asked.

"Don't smoke," I said eyeing her, shocked by her abruptness.

"Where ya from?" Magda said looking into my eyes.

"New York."

"So, wot ya doin' here, Girl?" she said. Then she was gone. She returned with a lighted spliff. She smoked it as though it was legal.

And then it began. Magda and I talked and talked and she became more intriguing to me as the night wore on. She had almond-shaped eyes and smooth dark almost black skin. Her hair was jet black, coarse and curly. She played tough, not smiling much. She kept a straight face.

"Do you have a boyfriend?" she asked when finally there was a lull in the conversation.

I didn't but I hated to admit it. "No. Do you?"

"No."

And that was that for a long time.

But there was something to the question that remained unanswered, despite both of our final answers. Magda had a mysterious way about her. She had been born in Egypt and her family moved to London when she was a child. Her father was an archaeologist. Her father was mean. That's all she would say about him.

"Mine too," I said.

"Why do you think they're so mean?" Magda asked me one night after we left Heaven and were standing outside the club. The sound of obnoxious boys were all around us. The sound of loud pop music got louder and quieter every time the door to Heaven opened and shut.

"Mine is mean because my mother died suddenly and he couldn't handle it."

"Your mum's dead?" Magda asked probingly.

"That's what I said."

"How? Did he kill her? You said he was mean."

"No. She's just dead, that's all. Why is your father so mean?"

"It's a long story. I'll tell you someday."

She never did.

And we met every weekend of my semester abroad and we never talked about our mean fathers again.

Her letter lay flat and perfect as the day that I opened the aerogramme the first time, as if it were sacred. We had written to each other incessantly after I left London in 1986. Her letters were an event. Her words leapt off the pages, begging for me to lap them up. She often spoke of things political, of which I was unfamiliar. She railed against the government and the status quo. She wrote of the pyramids burning. I was a simple American, not concerned with the implications of history, privilege and patriotism. Magda was always aware of things outside of the four walls of her existence. I had yearned to be like her, to care about the things she cared about, to say the things she said. I wished I could be in her head, with a mind that understood the bigger world. I listened harder when I was with her...but I couldn't comprehend her rage. I couldn't understand the need to protest or fight for something you believed in. I couldn't fathom terrorism or blind hatred in the name of religious conviction.

I had been stuffed away inside the brick walls of the Eastside Girls Academy where nothing significant to the rest of the world got in or came out. Magda opened the door to all the things that polite young women should never concern themselves with.

I re-opened the 20 year old aerogramme again, unfolding the thin paper.

My friend,

Egypt is burning and I wish I was there instead of sitting in London when I should be with my people. The police are burning down luxury hotels. They're sick of it. Shit salaries while the rich get richer. They change the laws everyday making it hard for the common man to abide by them. Something is amiss. The President is killing his own people. I wish I was with my people fighting or in the land of the free ignoring the rest of the world like you lot... ha ha! Bollocks!

Did you even hear about the riots?

Stay strong. Promise me.

Magdalene

ENTRY:

I will actually see Magda in a couple of days. What will I say to her? How will I begin to tell my story? Will she even care? How could I admit that I did everything she told me not to? Will she blame me for my pathos? Seeing her will remind me of what I was supposed to be.

Sleep was starting to crawl up my leg. My stomach was full and my fingers still sticky with mustard. I picked up the book from the desk, flicked the ceiling light off and folded myself beneath the reading lamp attached to the bed post. It was "You Can Heal Your Life," the book that Rene gave me and I had never finished reading. It was the book that the sick woman on the plane was reading. I glanced at the dog-eared page where I left off, skimming it as if it was the first time. With a distracted mind; I realized I had become bored with healing my life. I was distracted by thoughts of seeing Magda in a couple of days. My mind wandered between memories of her letters and the imminent return to my life as a mother with a child and a disease that I would tote around forever. I turned the pages of the book, gleaning nothing. Sleep had reached my neck, and I could barely keep my eyes open. I had forgotten to call Rain back, but I would call her tomorrow afternoon when she would just be waking up. S*he's just fine with Estelle.*

The glaring reading lamp warmed my face but I was too tired to reach up to turn it off. I turned my back on it and fell into a deep sleep.

It started as a mumble and became a roar.

"No he didn't die."

"No he didn't die..."

'No he couldn't die!"

"AAAAAAAAAAAAAAggGGGGG!" the sound that came out of my mouth woke me staring into the bright light that was blinding me.

I was trapped between sleepiness and consciousness.

I sat straight up in bed, relying on the headboard to keep me from falling off the bed. I heard myself saying out loud to the silence, "Not again." "Not again." "Not again." My hands clung to my face, shielding my eyes. I couldn't open them. I was shivering.

The nightmare had taken me right back to the brick wall of death. I re-felt that rumble in my stomach like the night that I punched the nurse who brought me the news of Marigold's death. I could see the blur of sad pale faces in my head all over again. In my ears sounded the buzz of the dispatcher's drone in the squad car. I heard my own last words to Peter, "you can't raise a child when you are one."

I let the silence and the peace of the room hold me. I lay still letting the waves inside me subside. This tumultuous place between a dream and what is real; what was real; what could have been real, again, shook me to the core. I let the room stop spinning on its own. I reached up and turned the reading light off. I fell back into the comfort of white cotton. I was feverish. My heart pounded.

I closed my eyes and pieced together the dream, trying to make sure that it had been a dream. My heart pounded as I recalled what my sub-conscious delivered. *But it was so real.*

"Are you the wife of Peter Holmes?" asked the officer.

"Yes, I am," I had stuttered.

"This is Officer William Landry of the Phoenix Police Department. I hate to inform you that there has been a bad accident. I'm sorry to inform you that Mr. Holmes has died."

"No he didn't die."

"No he didn't die"

"No he couldn't die."

"AAAAAAAAAAAAAAAggGGGGG!"

"Mrs. Holmes? Mrs. Holmes?" the officer had repeated into the phone.

"When did it happen? How did it happen? Why?" I had stumbled.

The officer persisted, "How soon can you get here? Where are you?"

"I can't get there. I'm on the other side of the world."

"What the hell are you doing there?" Roy's voice crashed in rudely interrupting the officer. "Ava, you're always running away… This is your fault."

"Mrs. Holmes, what will the late Mr. Holmes do?" the Officer said tauntingly. "Who will take care of his paperwork? Is there anyone that can be at the scene within the hour?"

My heart had stopped.

"I'm here." It was the accented voice of Veloris. The voice that I remembered that was bold enough to assure me that she was just Peter's friend.

"See Morgan, I told you, all that runnin' is no good. Look what you've done now…" It was Roy again.

I could hear the sound of Rain whimpering. "Rain!" I said aloud to the empty room. *Rain wasn't there. She was in America, Georgia, Atlanta, Estelle's house.*

I pushed my eyelids all the way open, forcing them to see what was real and not imagined. I forced myself to stand up, to steady myself. I pushed through all of the sheets and staggered across the hardwood floor to turn on the ceiling light. It was pitch black outside.

The storm in me finally broke, bringing me to my knees. I could no longer contain the weight. The dark grey rain cloud that I had been carrying around inside, finally burst. My whole body cried. My eyes were red and swollen. My throat hurt from the guttural growl coming from my core. My hands were sore from punching the mattress; down feathers fell to the floor like snow. I cried because I was missing everything. I yelled at the pristine bare walls, "I miss you!" I was crawling toward the bed, which seemed miles away.

My body was weak. The tantrum drained me. I missed Marigold, I missed Rain. I missed Peter. I missed so much that my stomach ached. Regrets clung to me like a snug fitting jacket. I crawled on to the side of the bed, praying intermittently and patiently watching each hour as the night's shadows turned to dawn.

When there was just enough light, I scrambled for my notebook. I scribbled in it:

ENTRY:

What am I running from? The need to stand still.

Eventually, there was a knock at the door. I was startled. It was Stacy. I could hear her outside the door, "Madame? Madame, are you OK? May I come in?"

I pretended that I didn't hear her, hoping that she would go away. But she persisted. "Madame, it's me, Stacy. Would you care for something to eat? I wanted to see if you were OK. There was quite a mess in the kitchen and I thought you had fallen ill?"

I had left a mess in the kitchen. I hoped that she wouldn't tell Allegra. *Stacy would report that I was an impolite house guest.* I groggily put my feet on the ground. I looked in the mirror. My eyes were bloodshot and swollen. There was still Honey Mustard on the edges of my lips. I wasn't ready to be seen. There were so many confidences that I needed Stacy to keep.

Through the door I spoke. "Stacy, I'm OK. I'm sorry for the mess. No, thank you for breakfast. I'm not hungry at all. Thank you. Thank you for everything. I will clean up the mess downstairs."

"Madame. No worries. It's early. It's breakfast time. I have already tidied up. Just wanted to check on you. It's my day off. Are you sure you have everything you need?"

"I do."

"Have a nice day. Look after yourself."

"I will."

I attempted to reach Rain again. They were not home. I'm sure Estelle had her out enjoying more precious moments that I would miss. *I was still learning how to unlove Peter, love me and her at the same time.*

What I needed most was to call Peter. I needed to confirm that he didn't die. I needed to hear his warm voice. I wanted him to know that I will always love him in some way just because of what we dared to try despite the facts of our differences. I didn't know what I would say when he would tell me he no longer loved me and that he loved *her*. And he would mean it. I couldn't kill him off, no matter how hard I tried. He would always be Rain's father. I owed Rain a father. I had failed her so many times already.

I had one day left in the countryside and then I would go to London to spend a few days with Magda, if she and I had any friendship left. Allegra booked a hotel room for me so I could see her. I feared we would meet that first evening and have only breaths between us. The excitement would have long ago faded. *Surely, letters could not sustain us.*

Allegra called to give me details on travel to London the next morning. Allegra's driver, Tom, would pick me up in the morning at 9 a.m. sharp, in order to get the 10:30 a.m. train into London. Paddington Station. Track 2. It would be easy to take the tube to the hotel in Earl's Court. The tube was walking distance to the hotel. Tom had all of the check-in information.

I had the whole rest of the day to myself. I could have done anything I wanted to do in the blue and white guest room on the second floor. I was free. I could have walked the gardens again, studying the petals of the flowers. Smelling their seductive scents. I could have snooped again. Peeking in cabinets, pulling out drawers, listening to the creak of old things that have remained shut for many years. I could have peeked in Hugh and Harvey's room searching for clues to parenting that I hadn't yet learned. I could have gone into the master suite, looking for evidence of marital dissatisfaction. I could have looked at Newlen's collection of classic Jazz albums. I could have laid in their empty king-size bed like I had laid in my own for so many nights, wishing it were smaller. I could have bathed in Allegra's expensive European soaps and sprayed myself with rare scents and pretended that this life was mine. *I could have.* I could have called Tom, the driver, to take me into town for souvenirs and Shepard's pie at the famous Stratford pub. I could have cried some more. However, I decided to do none of the above.

I decided to be still. To stay where I was. To write something from my blue and white room where there was peace and quiet.

CHAPTER 16 | *Bold Things*

London, England May, 1989

• • • **I**'*m always desperate to spill my guts to you. What is it about you...about us that fills me with such relief just knowing that you are out there in the world? So far away and so close to me at the same time. There's so much I want to tell you. Will you ever come back to London? When can we sit up and talk all night long like we did those nights outside of Heaven?*

Lots of love for you. Magdalene

London, England May, 2005

Magda met me at Masala Restaurant. I arrived early; nervous, I guess. We met in Trafalgar Square. I had studied my A-Z and had been eager to experience the strangeness of being an American in London once again. I had walked slowly from the tube to the restaurant and still arrived 15 minutes ahead of her. I ordered a drink; the money that Allegra had given me was burning my pocket. I hadn't spent any of it and I was leaving soon. I ordered a white wine spritzer, remembering that Rene assured me that one glass of watered down wine would not send me into a flare.

I was sitting at the bar with my back to the door and there was a firm tap on my shoulder. As if a balloon popped inside me, I felt a burst of excitement in my stomach. As I slowly turned, there she was, Magda, whose sneaky smile hadn't changed. Everything else about her seemed to have shifted. *Perhaps it was me.*

"You 'ave a light?" she asked me with an exaggerated cockney accent.

I tried to join her in the act; suspicious and shy like I was when we first met at Heaven. "Don't smoke," I said with a monotone. Within the second, we jumped to hug each other, me falling off of the bar stool, her wobbling, as we fell into a sloppy embrace.

I could smell her familiar smell of hand rolled cigarettes and exotic tobacco as we hugged. "It's so great to see ya girl," Magda said. She was thinner than I remembered. She wore a messy ponytail with strands hanging from all sides. Her hair was too long. She peered at my unkempt locks and saluted me with a "thumbs up." "I like your hair, sister!" she said almost too loudly. The maitre d' understood what we needed before we asked. He led us to a corner table lit only with a small candle's flame which diminished the years between us, illuminating only our joy. "Would you like a drink?" he asked Magda, as she eyed my half full spritzer.

She said, "I'll 'ave what she's 'aving." She turned to face the waiter and said, "This is my brilliant mate from America, Morgan. 'Avent seen in her in ages." She looked at me with adoring eyes.

The Indian waiter smiled at me and said, "I'll be right back."

Magda was desperately fussing with her hair. Her shaking hands couldn't seem to grasp the tufts of hair. The ponytail was lopsided and loose; the rubber band tattered. It seemed that she had developed a nervous tic. "So wot's up, girl?"

I was anxious as I reached into my bag. "I have something for you. It's a letter."

"Why? We're together, finally," she said, her face twisted with confusion.

"Letters are really all that we've had between us. I just wanted to— just read it," I said, not knowing the whys, just knowing that it felt like the best way to reach her.

Magda pulled her reading glasses from her bag. Her hands noticeably shook. Her reading glasses were black oversized ovals. They fit her face awkwardly, now that her face was smaller. She said apologetically, "I can't see a thing without them."

She took the letter from my hand, opened the envelope carefully and pulled out the letter that I had written from Allegra's guest room. Her face was serious as she skimmed the page for clues from this odd hand-delivered letter. The waiter had brought her drink. She took one shaky sip and rested the wine glass on the table. She read diligently, engrossed in each word.

While she read, I studied her face. She had aged. *We both had.* Fine lines decorated her face which was no longer plump and pleasing as it once was. Her skin, dark as night, was still smooth, only there was a smidgen of excessive skin forming jowls around her tiny lips. The excess skin was more evident when her head was down. The weight loss in her face was subtle but noticeable to one who had so carefully studied her first face. Magda had been tamed and tumbled by loss. I could see it in her eyes as they digested every word that bared my soul.

She read:

Dear Magda,

I know we promised each other independence. I failed. I fell into the pressure of the American dream; being happy, settled, and suburban. I married a man who had all the things that my heart ached for, back then. I had been motherless for too long. When Peter and I both revealed our true selves; we didn't like what we saw. We have a daughter whom we love madly but our family has fallen apart.

A year ago, I was diagnosed with Lupus which is like carrying a match around inside my body. It can ignite at any time. I am fragile. I'm afraid.

I haven't spoken to Peter in months. He found a new woman who has replaced me. Rain and I are living in Atlanta without a solid plan. All I have left is this path that you, unknowingly, set for me. Life can be so random.

I have to be honest. I have worried that this meeting wouldn't go well. I fear there hasn't been enough contact to establish the connection that we have built with only strong words and letters. When we met we were so innocent and unformed. All we had to give were words. We only revealed selected pieces of ourselves; I only hold pieces of you and I want more. We thought that these strands were love. Are they? How could they be?

So much has happened. I am here with you in the flesh and I can only hope that all these words that we have written mean something. I fear that our friendship is simply an illusion that can't withstand the flesh. Please tell me that it's real because truths are all I can take.

Once you wrote to me that you want to spill your guts to me. That phrase haunts me. I think of it often. Now is the time. I have much to share with you, too. And for some odd reason, I still feel more comfortable with you on paper.

I am hoping that our friendship can grow beyond letters. That we can leave the starkness of the blank page and finally connect. This will be my last letter and hopefully the start of much more.

Love, Morgan

Tears were falling from her eyes. A loud birthday celebration had started across the restaurant. Waiters were singing to an older Indian man whose face glowed in the light of many birthday candles. Magda spoke above the din, "Morgan, my father raped me when I was 16. He did it because he found out…"

My heart was speeding up. "Found out what?"

"About my girlfriend. He said I am a filthy abomination. He said he had to show me what if feels like to be with a man. He said he was teaching me to be a woman."

"Happy birthday to you and many more…." the waiters bellowed across the room.

"I'm so sorry, Magda. Why didn't you tell me? Why didn't you call? What happened next?" I stumbled with what to say. Her words shook me. Suddenly my tepid saga of chronic illness; a future of omnipresent exhaustion and battered kidneys seemed superfluous.

I sat uncomfortably on my ottoman that was covered in rich gold satin with large white flowers. Magda seemed to hang off hers, needing stability. I sat awkwardly through our silence, my knees starting to tighten.

"What could you've done about it if I'd called you? It's just my life. I guess your illness is now your life. It was silly for me not to share what happened. I couldn't bear to talk about it."

"Where is Musim now?" Her father's name meant "belief," she had told me once in a letter.

"They're still married but both dead to me. They believe that what he did was for my own good. He says it was an act of religious conviction.

"Were the police involved?" I asked.

"A family's honor means more than the law. I could have been killed if anyone found out, to save the family name. He would have only been "slapped on the wrist," is that what Americans call it? It wasn't worth it for any of us to tell. I try to forget it and find peace in other places. Like with you."

"I'm here for you," I said.

"They got me a flat. They're paying for my amnesia. He's never to come near me again. I've been taking anti-depressants since I was 18. They make me depressed, I can't hold onto a real job. I freelance when I can."

...Solitude is no longer what I want. Where are you when I need you? How are things in America? Have you gone off to become someone's wife? Someone's mother? Someone who has to abide by the rules? Calm my nerves. Let me know that you are still you. With love,

Magdalene

"You were right. I did stop writing to you because I was ashamed that I had become typical. I was living a life without imagination, as we used to say."

"We also used to say when shit happens, use it for art. That's the only thing to do with it," Magda said.

"How is your writing coming?" I asked.

"That's the only thing I have to show for myself is a book of erotic poems that saved my life."

The waiter interrupted again. "Would you care for starters?"

Without looking up, in unison we said, "No thanks."

"The pill I take runs off with my appetite," Magda explained. "I'm not hungry much. I hope you don't mind."

Bits and pieces of her letters kept coming to me as I looked at her face, seeing the mature pain that looked like teenaged angst before.

...your letters excite me. This is a very indulgent love that we share. It's a big love for such a small space in time. How did you do that to me? Write soon. I am on the edge of my seat, thinking of you always,

Magdalene

"It's been a lonely year," I started.

"You were married so you weren't really alone," said Magda.

"Sometimes marriage can be the loneliest place," I said.

"How's the Warden?" Magda asked without hesitation, using that unfortunate nickname that I had given Roy. The name hit me like a bullet every time I heard it from lips other than my own.

"I don't call him that anymore," I said to assuage my guilt. "He's fine. He's 78. He's mad at me because I'm here. He says I'm careless and self-absorbed."

"Why are you in London, anyway?"

"I came over because my friend, Allegra from Eastside Girls Academy, wanted to do something for me…It's really incredible. She was with me the night my mother died in 8th grade. It's an intricate friendship. You know how Girls' schools can be."

Magda replied, "I don't know anymore. I've lost touch with my friends from school. After *it* happened, I couldn't pretend. So, you and your husband are splittin' up? I'm gutted to hear that. I regretted saying what I said about you getting married all those years ago. I was just angry that you were growing up without me. I wanted to be like you. You seemed so level-headed, Morgan."

"Magda, I always wanted to be like you. Not so level-headed."

We sat in silence. I drained my second glass of wine in one gulp. She summoned our waiter with a raised finger to bring her another spritzer.

"Well, at least we are together again," Magda finally said.

"But not for long. You know I have to get back to my daughter, Rain."

"What's it like? Being a mother? I imagine it's dreadful," she said lazily with her drink at her lips.

"It's hard." The tears appeared in the corners of my eyes. "It's the only time in my life that I can actually feel my soul. Mothering rips you out of yourself. Our self is all we have, until we birth a child. My little girl's whole life depends on me now. Every move I make she is touched in some way, inside and out. I know that somewhere above, score is being kept. I so want to do this right."

"What a beautiful thing to say about something so horrifying. I never want kids. Can't take the pressure." Magda said.

"You could take it. It's almost necessary."

"Bloody hell, Morgan, I'm too shallow for kids. Make-believe is my job. I couldn't deal with being needed so much."

"You've dealt with more real stuff than most people could take. You're just dealing with it in your own way."

"That's why I love you, girl. *You* understand me."

"Being sick has knocked the wind out of me. I hope Rain will understand *me* someday. I'm across the world without her. I could have brought her. Allegra said it was okay. I chose not to. I was being selfish one last time. I really need to go back and face the fact that I'm someone's mother. I can only hope that Rain will forget all the things that I haven't done for her."

"Do you really think that score is being kept?" Magda asked.

Magda was finally hungry. We had left Masala and walked like we used to around Trafalgar Square. The young hip boys were still there, dancing and singing for attention from strangers. Magda had suggested we go for fish and chips like we used to. We waited in a rowdy line for too long and then I paid with a handful of pound coins, glad to finally have someone to give them to. When we got the sheer paper bags in our hands spilling with steaming chips and deep fried cod, we ate with our fingers. There was salt and vinegar everywhere and heat was penetrating our palms. We had relaxed into our old rhythm. Being with her felt like it had before everything happened.

"My flat is not too far from here. It's just at Charing Cross. I want to give you a copy of my book of poems. It's dedicated to my ex-girlfriend, Lorna. The one that my father found out about. The one that..." her voice fell off.

"Say no more."

We tossed the grease-soaked bags in a trash bin outside of a row of pubs, spilling with drunken middle-aged men. We sucked the last vestiges of vinegar and salt off our fingers. We needed to go back to her flat to clean up. *I prayed that the fried food wouldn't do anything to me.*

As she put the key into the lock, Magda said, "You can go to the loo first. When I emerged from her bathroom, she ran past me screaming, "Gotta go bad. Make yourself at home!" I looked around for the light switch. I flicked it on. The walls were bare and painted black.

Magda's flat was a tiny studio space that took up only a corner of a huge brick building. On the small round dining table sat a box of letters that was labeled *Morgan*.

"Don't these black walls depress you?" I yelled into the bathroom. She didn't answer.

I saw the box that said *Morgan*. It was full of my letters. I was curious about all the things that I had written to her. I was afraid to read those words and feelings that had bound us together for so long. I still had my box of her letters but hadn't had the courage to open it again.

"The walls are actually quite soothing, I find." Magda said as she stepped out of the bathroom.

"I am honored that you saved my letters."

"According to your latest letter, I should throw them away now, right?"

"No. That's not what I meant. We should just do more than just write our friendship. Let's really have it."

I could feel the ticking of the clock, pushing me to go, but I was compelled to stay for just a little while longer. Wanting and needing something to *happen* to make the letters finally mean something.

Magda was nervous. We both were. She stood up and said, "Drink?" The small icebox was right in front of us. "All I have is vodka and water in there."

I wasn't thirsty. I needed to leave soon. She poured herself a drink in a small glass. It was mostly water with just a sprinkle of vodka. "Can't take my pills and drink too much," she said. "You're sure you don't want a drink?"

"No thanks. I take pills, too."

"I'll get your book." She walked just a few feet to a door. It was a closet that had been converted into a library. All it held were book shelves. One shelf had only copies of her little red book.

She pulled out a red pen from her pocket. She opened the inside cover of the book to write.

"What are you writing?" I asked.

"Something to you."

It was really time to go.

She finished her inscription. I commenced the closing ceremonies. *I came only for the book.* The two-cheeked goodbye kiss shifted. When I kissed her second cheek, I held on for a second longer than usual. I aimed my lips to the center of her warm moist mouth. I could still taste the salt. I lingered there for a moment to get a read from her. It had been over a decade of incomplete sentences. It had been over a decade since distance had robbed us of this connection. We had seduced each other with hungry words and shared angst.

Something outside of myself made me reach for Magda's breast, I whispered in her ear, "Is it okay?"

She welcomed me. She kissed me back and we both forgot all that we had been through, just for a moment.

...I thought I was in love. It was just a passing fancy. I'm writing poems to recover. Why aren't you writing to me? Telling me of your life. Is there something that I should know? Wishing I had more memories of you.

I send you lots of kisses. Wet kisses.

Magdalene

We kissed as if time had not been invented. I kissed her neck and ran my fingers through her messy dark hair. It was soft, despite its tangled look. I pushed the neckline of her sweater down so I could celebrate the teardrop tattoo that was emblazoned on her upper arm. I found her lips again and my mouth came undone. My tongue found hers and we shivered at the electricity of finding each other in the darkness.

..hating for this letter to end... Life calls me back to my four walls. Write soon with more of your magic. -Magdalene

Magda had begun undressing me and kissing the tops of my ample breasts. My nipples came alive with the feel of her wet tongue. My hand had clumsily found her zipper on her black jeans and my fingers pulled it down, effortlessly. Her body was perfect; fragile and strong. I nervously placed my warm hand into the oasis below. Her hair was abundant and soft there. Magda was starting to quietly quake at my slight touch, leaving a hint of wetness on my fingertips.

I felt my mouth opening again. My lips and tongue were swollen with anticipation, yearning to have more of her. She agreed silently and we both fell softly onto her twin mattress. We were wrapped in the embrace of past words. I wanted to wash her clean of shame and the ugliness of religious lies. Magda teased me all over with her tongue. I felt myself drowning in her.

"We can't do this," Magda said forcefully. She was suddenly upright; her hair was messier, her clothes askew. She re-zipped her jeans, attempted to smooth her unruly hair and kissed me ever so lightly on my lips. "This can't be right. This will complicate everything, Morgan. I have always loved you. *Not* sexually. Bigger than that," she said softly.

I touched her hair. I let silence blossom between us.

"You're right, Magda. You're right. This is complicated. I have to leave now."

But just for those few moments with Magda, I remembered how passion unearths things that have been buried. I had forgotten the power of two fingers and a shower of kisses.

I looked at the clock again. *It was time.* Magda walked me to the elevator. We said our goodbyes and farewells and see-you-soons in the dimly lit hallway. She kissed me tenderly on my forehead like a parent kisses her child. She gently pushed me into the elevator, tears streaming down her cheeks. I was sad to leave her but ready for Rain. The elevator sank to the ground floor slowly. Her book was entitled, "Bold Things." Her red inked message was: "To Morgan with rejuvenated love."

Score is being kept.

CHAPTER 17 | *Found*

Atlanta, Georgia May, 2006

It's been exactly fourteen months, four days and 9 hours since so much of our life was washed away by a single mechanical failure. Everything we had was swept away with the tide of a past life. It's been exactly thirteen months since Peter and I walked away from a "dream house" and I moved everything we had left to Atlanta, Georgia. It seems like a lifetime since we walked away from each other like zombies; numb and cold. We were refugees fleeing from something life-threatening; our marriage. It's been almost one year, eight days and 13 hours since I left London; since I dreamed that Peter died; since Magda and I kissed, and that my body went, officially, into remission.

A friend of Dorian's rented the place that we call home to Rain and me. It's clean and quaint and is just big enough to hold the meager belongings that we can still call our own. When we need new things, we shop at Goodwill where others have unloaded their excess, hoping to feel less guilty about their insatiability. We used to go there to give, now we go there to receive. *What a difference a day makes.*

I have comfortably settled into the torment of my malady. Each day is a new adventure. One day my top lip swells like a tire, taut and plump, spreading from east to west across the planes of my face. Other days my fingers are so stiff and swollen, I can't write, type, or open the peanut butter jar for Rain. Some mornings, I rise with sand in my veins pulling me back into bed. On those days, I whisper to Rain, "Today, Mama must sleep," and she crawls into bed with me, clumsily stroking my head with her miniature caress. On those days, I allow the TV to do what I can't; entertain her and make her feel joy. Some mornings, I wake up ugly. Those are the nights my cheeks have become inflamed; raw and leathery to the touch. Those are the nights that the wolf bites, reminding me that I am never fully out of the woods. I slather expensive steroidal creams on my temporary wounds, trying not to scratch them while I pray for relief. *Was it something I ate?* After a day or two, prednisone sends the wolf back into the woods.

To the naked eye, I'm "fine." The shocks within sleep more than ever. I now live ever so carefully, hoping not to awaken them. No one would know from looking at me how much I've had to endure. *So much of it happened on the inside.*

It's been exactly two days and 3 hours since I called Peter. I had to. I had to know that he was on earth, whether he was speaking to us or not. When I heard his voice, I sighed with relief that the nightmare could finally stop taunting me. I had carried that dream in my mind every waking hour since leaving England. It's still so vivid: waking up in Allegra's house, alone and frightened at the thought that Peter was dead.

"Peter, it's me. Don't hang up. Please," I had said. I was sitting in the borrowed leather rocking chair that Estelle had loaned us but said we could keep. I was staring out the window at the rain. All I could hear was the sound of it dripping off the roof.

I was the only one with anything to say.

"Peter, I had a dream about you. You died in a car accident. I woke up shaken and scared. Your death didn't soothe me the way I wished it would. It was like losing a part of myself all over again."

The distant buzz and ping of the phone's connectivity was the only sound.

"Peter, I don't know what you're feeling. I guess I have never known. Getting married was a mistake. I don't want to be mad anymore. Rain needs her father. Please say something, Peter."

His voice hadn't changed. It was still deep and warm. His voice finally filled my ears after all of his silence. "Morgan, you're right," he said. "We've made a mess."

Silence. *There must be more for him to say.*

"Morgan, I never wanted to leave New York. It was the first time in my life that I felt alive and free. I've hated you for that."

"Why did you go along with it, then?"

"You said it would make you happy. I wanted to make you happy." His voice crackled..

"Why didn't you tell me how you *felt* about it?" I asked.

"What could I have said? You had it all planned out. You couldn't have heard me anyway. You were like a crazy person. You were so driven to go and to make a life for us that you forgot that I was a part of it. Besides, I never knew how to say what I felt. I did as I was taught: say nothing, feel nothing, let God handle it. You know I grew up with a muzzle on."

"Peter, I just wanted what you had. A family of my own."

"And, I wanted what *you* had: to know about the world. *An education*. Now we are both left with less than we started with.

"We have more. We have Rain," I said.

"I did manage to get something. I finally graduated."

"I'm proud of you."

"What matters is that Rain will be proud of me."

"A degree won't make her proud. You being in her life will." I couldn't resist. "Is *she* still there? In your life, I mean."

"What do you want me to say to that?"

"The truth."

"Yes. She is."

"I don't understand how you could love someone else so quickly. Don't you ever think about us and what we were trying to be?"

"It got hard for me to love you. And I'm so sorry for that. You had become unrecognizable to me when you were sick. You had given up."

"No, *you* gave up on me!"

"It all happened so fast. You had become a stranger, so weak and scared. I was scared, too. I ran. I ran to someone who was there to catch me. Someone who could help me forget."

"That's how things happen: fast. Life has no timing. Life is not courteous. What would you do if I died and Rain got sick? Or if *she* did?"

"I don't know," he whispered.

"She should know that you run away when there's trouble. If I had known that little detail, none of this would have happened. I would have left you in the airport."

"I didn't even know it about myself. I hope it won't ever happen again. I don't want to hurt anyone else. Especially not Rain. "

"Staying is what matters in life. Hope is flimsy, Peter."

"Hope is all that some people have to hold on to."

"How disappointing life is. I don't want Rain to grow up with a muzzle over her mouth or blinders covering her eyes. She needs to know how to survive when life disappoints. I don't want her walking around in a religious haze hoping and waiting for God to take care of everything. That's just nonsense. It's for the mentally crippled. I want her to know how to take responsibility for herself."

"So, you don't believe in God anymore?"

"I do believe, but not in a manufactured God who leads people to believe they no longer have responsibility for themselves or their actions. You know I'd never been a follower until I met you. You and your God had me seduced for a minute there. Until I realized that all those years in church with a personalized Bible never gave you what you really needed, after all. I never want to believe in something that lets me down like you did. "

"I hope you don't make our little girl cynical, like Roy made you."

"I hope I don't make her motherless like Marigold made me. Roy just wanted me to be a realist. Not to lie to others and never to myself. It's a harder life but it doesn't leave you so empty. Will you ever come see Rain?"

"I want to. But I don't know what I'd say. She's nearly two years older. I'm so ashamed that I have disappeared from her life."

"You'll know what to say. She'll even know what to say to you. You're her *father*. She'll remember your touch and your smell."

"I wasn't ready to talk to you. Morgan, this is not easy for me. I've let everyone down. Especially you. Aunt Gladys is disgusted. Rain doesn't know me and all I have is—"

"Her? You have Rain, Peter. I didn't call to make you feel bad. We have all felt bad enough."

After a long pause, he said, "Besides finishing school, I finally got my act together and filed. You'll get some papers in the mail. It's the saddest thing I've ever done."

"It may be the most important thing you've ever done. You need to be free to find yourself. It's important for both of us. We need to go our separate ways. Rain will always connect us. I look forward to seeing who you will become."

"Same here." Peter asked cautiously, "Is there anyone new in your life?"

"Yes," I said.

"I hope you're happy," he said.

"Strangely, I am."

I am involved with a new lover. She cares for me like no one ever has. At night she smoothes coconut lotion on all the places that itch. She forgives me. She knows everything about me. She tolerates my horrid scratching, sometimes until my skin bleeds. She understands. She's always gentle with me. In the mornings, she always greets me with gratitude that we are still here. Every morning we breathe in the intoxicating aroma of Magnolia trees and red clay. This is the place where we belong. We are thankful.

When she rolls over, she eyes the clock, touches my skin, knowing when it's time for me to wake Rain, make her breakfast, get her ready and drive her to daycare. When I return, I go to my office in the front of our tiny house and look online for work. There are not a lot of recording studio jobs for a woman like me: a little frail, uncertain, and out of the loop. I have become a dinosaur while the big world kept spinning.

Rain and I have a mother-daughter life that holds us in like a cashmere sweater. As I drive her to daycare, I sing songs in the car and she claps. I bellow made-up songs about how much I love her. During the days when I'm at my computer, trying to piece together a ravaged career, I'm distracted by thoughts of her. I sit wishing the five hours would pass more quickly, so I can hold her hand and make up for all of that sick time.

I'm stronger now. I lift Rain into her car seat with ease. She insists that I lift her imaginary friend, too. They seem to love and depend on each other. I envy such a friendship, even an imaginary one. So many of my own friends have gone. For some, it was too much trouble having a sick friend. Magda and I do speak on the phone often. The time zones are no longer our issue. *We are friends who love bigger than that.* I still speak to Rene sometimes. She and Bethany live together and are thinking of adopting a child. She sends me text messages and emails to check on me. Her words are happy and healthy. All of the original Healthy Girls have stayed away. I am a constant reminder of how a good life can go bad.

When I pick Rain up from daycare, I want to run to her, take her in my arms and smother her with my love. In the evenings, I always prepare a proper dinner to make up for all those missed dinners. Her favorite meal is spaghetti with red sauce. I can't share it with her but I wish I could. *Tomato sauce is inflammatory.*

I can hear her voice even when she's not with me. We don't scream anymore. We sing. On sunny days, if I'm up to it, I take her to the park. Rain loves to run on the grass, through the trees, over the pebbles and stones. I can't keep her shoes on. She loves to take them off wherever she is. She's always losing a shoe. She craves freedom. *We all do.*

When Rain gets to grade school, her teachers will remind constantly, "Don't run!" I won't have to say it at all. She'll grow to understand what running can't do.

I have lost my mother figure. Gladys wants to love me, but that can't last because life will move on. Peter will someday marry again and Gladys will have to love the new one like she had to love me. I'll miss Gladys and her mothering. I'll even miss her attempts to make me more like her: gentler, kinder, and vapid. Maybe, I didn't need another mother, after all. Marigold is always within.

Today, I lay bare. I once was swept away by a flood of illusions. My eyes can see clearly now. I want to show Rain how to live the kind of life that will make her proud of *herself.* I live everyday showing Rain that what Rene Harden said is true: "You're a big girl from New York. You'll get home."

And I did.

$\mathcal{B}$ook $\mathcal{C}$lub $\mathcal{Q}$uestions

1. How have you dealt with the news of a friend's illness?

2. How did it make you feel?

3. Did you immediately offer the number of someone with the same illness?

4. Is it possible to replace a mother? If one does, does it create guilt? Why?

5. Why do you think that divorce is so prevalent with women who become ill?

6. Who are your favorite characters and why?

7. Who are your least favorite characters and why?

8. What is the significance of the cover art?

9. Do you think that divorce is "the right thing to do" when there are children involved? Why or why not?

10. How has Aunt Gladys been impacted by the death of her husband?

11. Did you think that Morgan was wrong to engage in intimacy with Kweku? Have you ever made a risky choice? Why? Why not?

12. What were the reasons that Morgan decided she didn't want to build a relationship with Kweku?

13. What is the significance of Magda and Morgan's relationship through letters?

14. Do you have any close friends that you never see and only write? Do you consider it a real friendship? Why or why not?

15. Do you believe in holistic medicines and therapies? What has your experience been?

16. What role does music play in the story? What role does music play in your own life?

17. What do you think Morgan was running from?

18. What is the significance of "You're a big girl from New York, you'll get home"?

19. Who is Morgan's lover at the end of the book?

20. Why is the book called "Hallucination"?

21. What is Morgan's relationship with God in the story? How does it differ from your own?

Seafoam Flesh

Vulnerable and humbled is what Kim Green saw in this moving portrait of a woman bared, which is why she chose this soul stirring image for the cover of hallucination.

"*Seafoam Flesh*"

Painting by D. Lammie-Hanson

"Seafoam Flesh" Limited Edition Giclee

The artwork, "*Seafoam Flesh*" by artist D. Lammie-Hanson is available in limited edition giclee, edition size of 125. Image size 15 X 30, printed with archival ink on archival acid-free rag premium paper and will be signed and numbered by D. Lammie-Hanson.

For additional information on how to purchase a limited edition giclee of "*Seafoam Flesh*" or other original work by D. Lammie-Hanson please contact the artist's representative:

Richard Beavers

House of Art

373 Lewis Ave

Brooklyn, NY 11233

Email: rbeavers@nychouseofart.com

www.nychouseofart.com

Phone 347-663-8195

*A*cknowledgements

Intense gratitude to all who have helped me write this book. No words are big enough to express how I feel about your help, your encouragement and your belief in me. I am so grateful that there are so many people who deserve an individual thank you, but space will not allow.

Agnes Hunter for giving me time to write. My surrogate family, the Calhouns, for inviting us in and letting us stay. To DJ Nature for his family, a roof, your enthusiastic belief and cruise control. Carol Lee Lorenzo, my fellow Callanwolde classmates and the countless additional editors. I want to especially thank Nancy Shulins, the comma queen, additional critique groups, countless readers and re-readers for your patience, tough words and belief that it could happen someday. And thanks to Cynthia Counts for your important advice. To the UUCA Women Writers for your love and commitment to your own words. To my UUCA friends and family in faith.

To Reverend Marti Keller for your love and support of me and your deep commitment to our craft.

To D. Lammie Hanson for giving *hallucination* a stunning face.

To Kelli Sae for giving Morgan the perfect song.

To Joann Vitelli for being a facemaker.

To Jim deBarros for your bottomless commitment and to Patrick Malloy for your assistance with the design.

To Sheila Mari for putting me in the 21st Century.

To Mimi Shroeder for making things happen.

To Melissa Standing, Vivian Chew, Uncle Rain and Michelle McCleary for your early enthusiasm, encouragement and loving words.

To Ayo Yetunde and her family for belief and just being here.

To Sasha Carter for 40 precious years of being Kings.

To Laurie Renfro for being one of a few who also have none...

To Lamoy for being an awesome father.

To the Sawyer family for always claiming me.

To my Cincinnati family above and below: I never forget.

To the Claydon family for your radical hospitality.

To CG wherever you are...

To Nordia Lee for you know why.

About the Author

Photo By Joann Vitelli

Kim Green ghostwrote "Life Is Not a Fairytale," the autobiography of *American Idol* winner, Fantasia Barrino, which became a Lifetime Television movie. The book was listed on both the New York Times and Wall Street Journal's Bestseller Lists. Kim Green is a featured author in the African American serial novel, "When Butterflies Kiss" (published by Silver Lion Press) and a contributor to "Proverbs for the People" (Dafina Books). As well, Kim co-wrote the Last Poets book, "On a Mission: Selected Poems and a History of The Last Poets. (Henry Holt). Kim's essay, "In the Absence of Blood" was featured in the anthology, "Who's Your Mama?" (Soft Skull Press). Kim Green's work has appeared in *Essence*, *The Source*, *Mode*, *American Baby*, *The Philadelphia Tribune*, *Paper*, and international publications, *i-D* and *The Wire*. Kim has interviewed countless recording artists including legends; *Patti Labelle, Al Jarreau, Mary J. Blige, Queen Latifah, Rickie Lee Jones and Tupac Shakur*.

Kim's creative words studio, WORDS, LLC, is based in Atlanta, Georgia.

hallucination is her first novel.

All correspondence should be sent to:

Kim Green

P.O. Box 941876

Atlanta, Georgia 31141

hallucinationthenovel.com

Blog: Kimgreenwords.tumblr.com